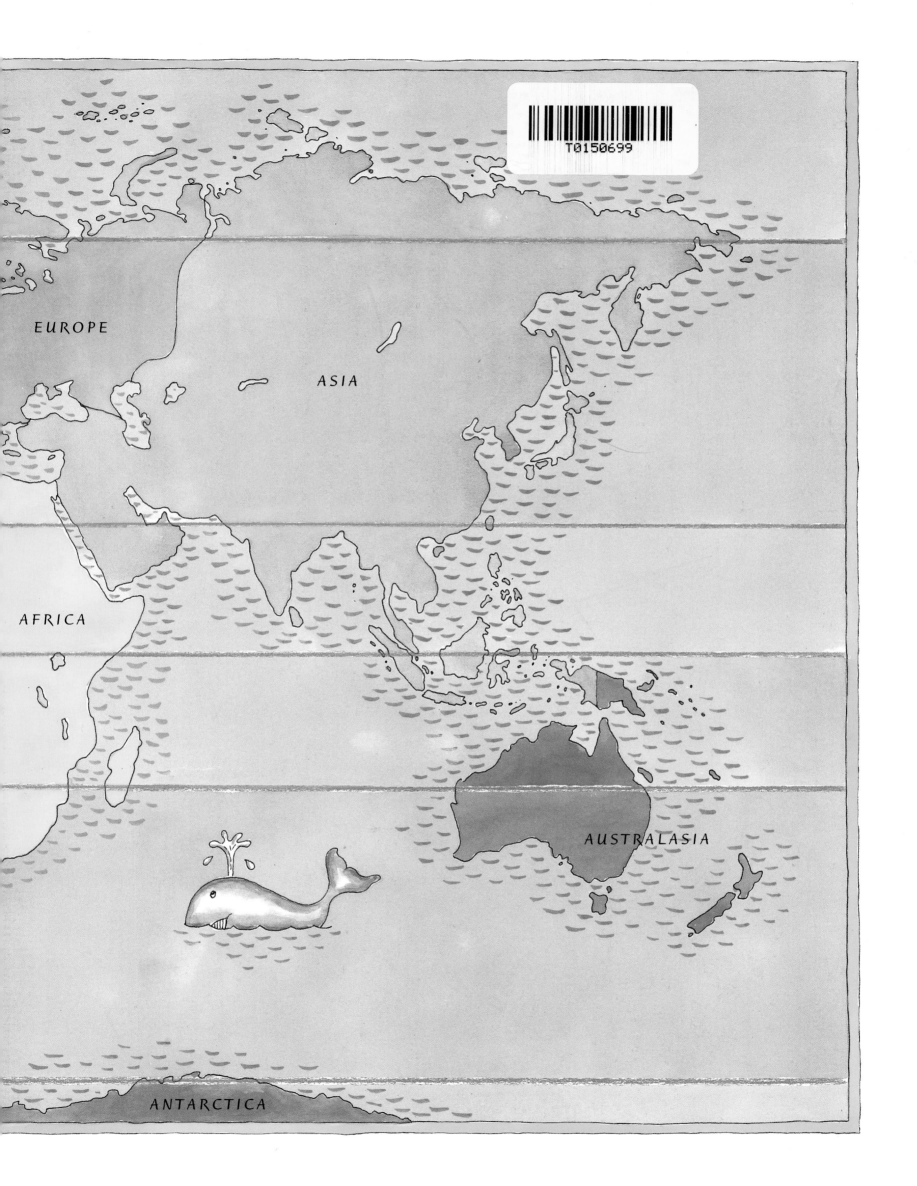

This edition is published by Armadillo, an imprint of Anness Publishing Ltd,
108 Great Russell Street, London WC1B 3NA; info@anness.com

www.armadillobooks.co.uk; www.annesspublishing.com; twitter: @Anness_Books

If you like the images in this book and would like to investigate using them
for publishing, promotions or advertising, please visit our website
www.practicalpictures.com for more information.

A CIP catalogue record for this book is available from the British Library.

Publisher: Joanna Lorenz
Editorial Consultant: Jackie Fortey
Consultants: Keith Lye and Michael Chinery
Project Editor: Belinda Wilkinson
Designer: Nigel Soper

Thanks to Isabel Clark

PUBLISHER'S NOTE
The author and publishers have made every effort to ensure that this book
is safe for its intended use, and cannot accept any legal responsibility or liability
for any harm or injury arising from misuse.

Manufacturer: Anness Publishing Ltd,
108 Great Russell Street, London WC1B 3NA, England
For Product Tracking go to: www.annesspublishing.com/tracking
Batch: 0163-22663-1127

My Big Book of the WORLD

Angela Royston ❖ Gerald Hawksley

ARMADILLO

CONTENTS

THE EARTH IN SPACE

8

WHAT IS A MAP?

9

HOW TO READ THE MAPS

10

CANADA AND ALASKA

12

UNITED STATES OF AMERICA

14

CENTRAL AMERICA

16

SOUTH AMERICA

18

WESTERN EUROPE

20

BRITISH ISLES

22

EASTERN EUROPE

24

NORTHERN EUROPE

26

in a house . . .   in a street . . .   in a town . . .   in a state . . .

Let's see where we live.

CONTENTS

NORTHERN AFRICA
28

SOUTH AFRICA
30

RUSSIA AND NORTHERN ASIA
32

SOUTHWEST ASIA
34

SOUTHERN AND SOUTHEAST ASIA
36

CHINA AND JAPAN
38

AUSTRALASIA
40

ARCTIC AND ANTARCTIC
42

SOME FLAGS OF THE WORLD
44

COUNTRY INDEX
45

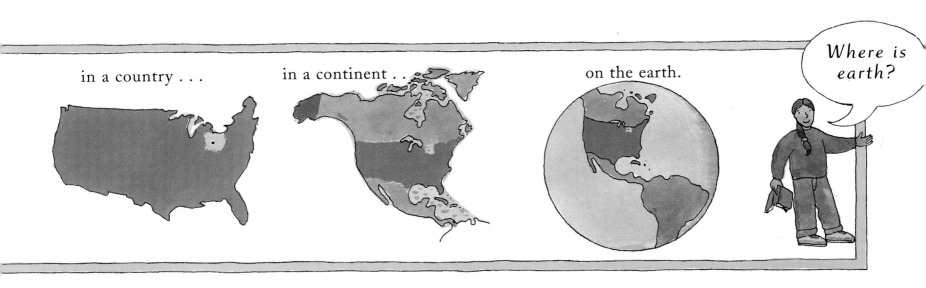

in a country . . .   in a continent . . .   on the earth.   Where is earth?

THE EARTH IN SPACE

The Earth is one of eight planets that spin around the hot Sun. The Moon spins around the Earth. The Sun is millions of miles away but it gives us light and heat.

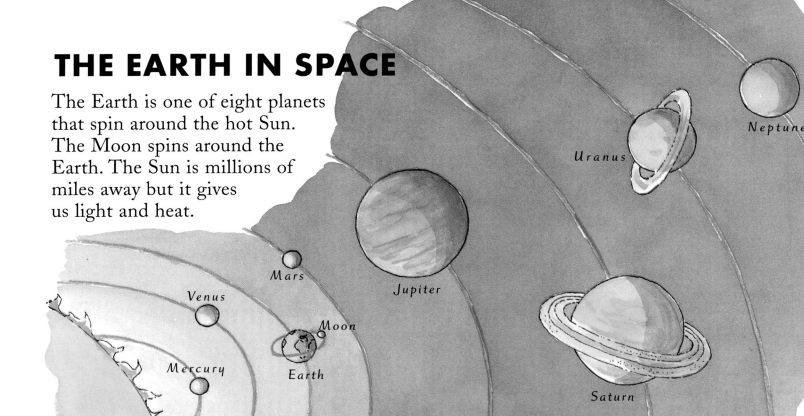

NIGHT AND DAY

The Earth is like a spinning top with the North Pole at the top and the South Pole at the bottom. Each spin takes 24 hours and, at any time, half the Earth is in daylight while the other half is in darkness.

So, as the Earth turns, you move from day into night and back into day again.

THE SEASONS

When the southern half of the globe leans towards the Sun, the north is darker and colder – it is winter.

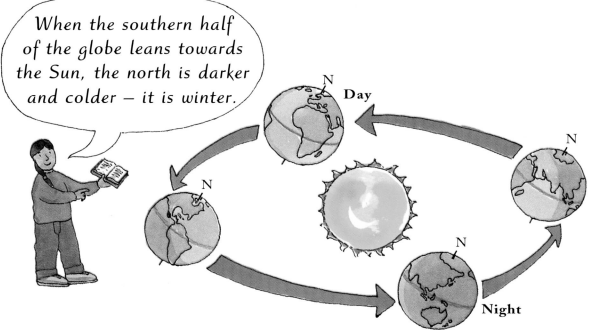

The Earth takes one year to orbit the Sun. The Equator is an imaginary line around the middle of the Earth. The Sun always shines strongly here and it is always hot. The Earth, however, is tilted. When the southern half leans towards the Sun, the days there are longer and hotter. It is summer.

Globe

WHAT IS A MAP?

The most accurate way to show the land and the oceans is to make a round model of the Earth, called a globe. Then you can see where each country is and how big it is.

Most maps show flat pictures of the Earth. But how do map-makers turn a round ball into a flat rectangle? They either cut zigzags around the North and South Poles or they stretch the land there to fill the gaps.

Try it yourself next time you peel an orange. Keep the peel in one piece and lay it flat.

Some maps look like peeled orange skin.

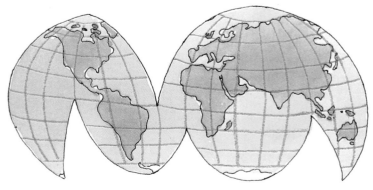

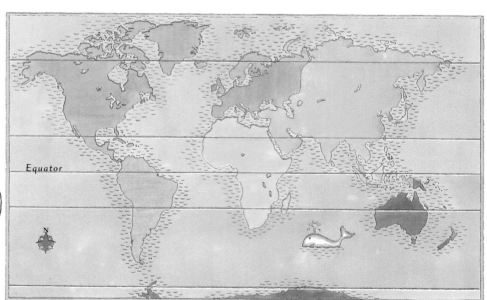

Equator

Look for these other imaginary lines on the maps in the book.

The Equator is an imaginary line around the Earth.

COMPASS ROSE

Maps are usually drawn with north at the top and south at the bottom. This means that east is usually on the right and

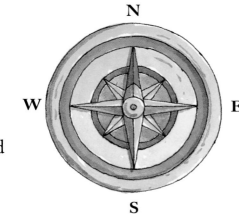

N

W   E

S

west on the left. The compass rose on each map shows exactly where north is.

HOW TO READ THE MAPS

If you floated over the Earth in a balloon, the land below would change from farmland to mountains, deserts, forests and ice. Sometimes you would float over big cities, sometimes over lakes and rivers. The higher you were, the bigger the area you would see at once. Look at our maps to find out what kind of landscape you would see.

Desert

Mountains

Tropical rainforest

Grassland or prairie

Woodland and farmland

Pine forest

Tundra and ice

If you were in a balloon, you would not know where you were unless you had a map. Only the map tells you the names of the countries, rivers, mountains and cities. It shows the borders between different countries. Look for these symbols and names on each map:

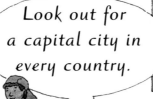

Look out for a capital city in every country.

Bucharest
Capital city

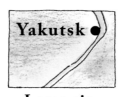
Yakutsk
Large city

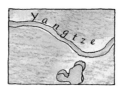
MALI
Country border

MISSOURI
State border

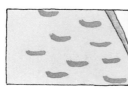
Yangtze
River and lake

Sea or ocean

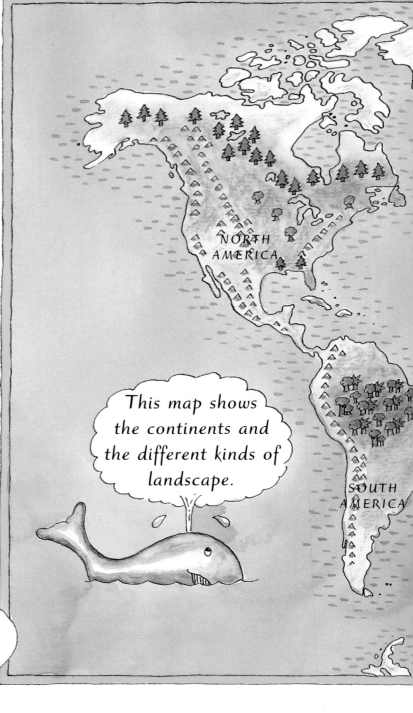

This map shows the continents and the different kinds of landscape.

NORTH AMERICA

SOUTH AMERICA

UNITED KINGDOM

NETHERLANDS

Amsterdam
Rotterdam

London

Brussels
BELGIUM
Lille

CHANNEL

Paris
Seine

Rennes

Loire

10

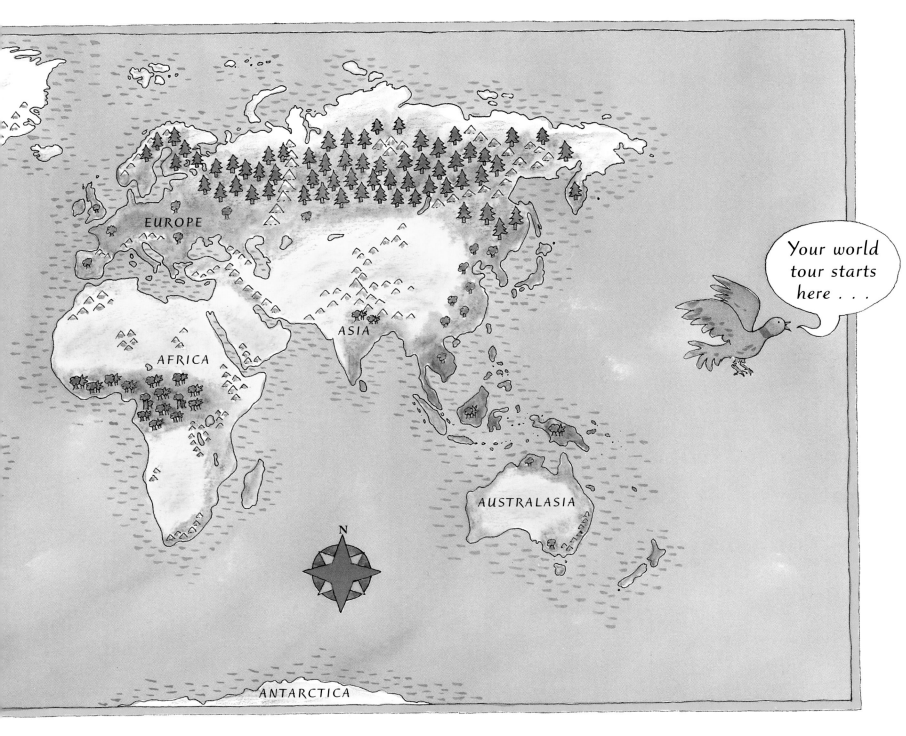

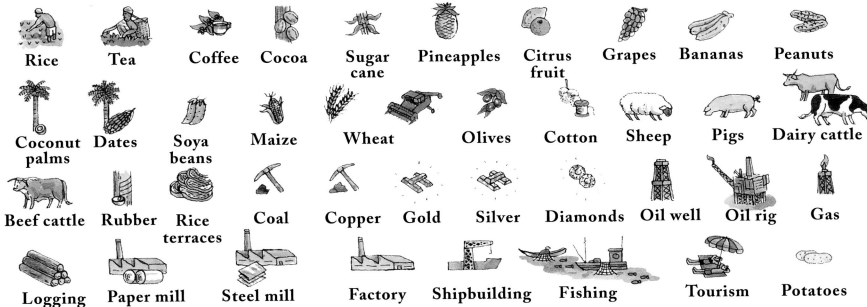

Rice	Tea	Coffee	Cocoa	Sugar cane	Pineapples	Citrus fruit	Grapes	Bananas	Peanuts
Coconut palms	Dates	Soya beans	Maize	Wheat	Olives	Cotton	Sheep	Pigs	Dairy cattle
Beef cattle	Rubber	Rice terraces	Coal	Copper	Gold	Silver	Diamonds	Oil well	Oil rig	Gas
Logging	Paper mill	Steel mill	Factory	Shipbuilding	Fishing	Tourism	Potatoes

Here are some of the pictures you will see on many of the maps.

11

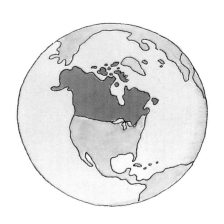

CANADA and Alaska

Canada is the second largest country in the world. It stretches from the Rocky Mountains in the west to the Atlantic Ocean. The land in the far north is always covered with snow. Many wild animals live here and in the forests. Most of the people live in the south, and work in the big cities, near the border with the United States of America.

Can you see?

Niagara Falls   **a lighthouse**   **a totem pole**   **an Inuit**

an ice hockey player   **a Mountie**   **a caribou**

a maple tree and leaf   **a beaver**   **a snow goose**

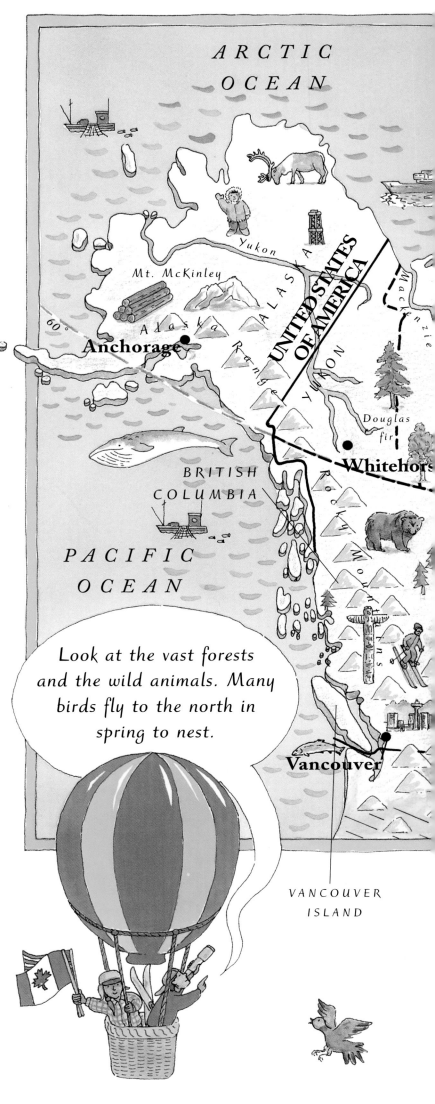

Look at the vast forests and the wild animals. Many birds fly to the north in spring to nest.

12

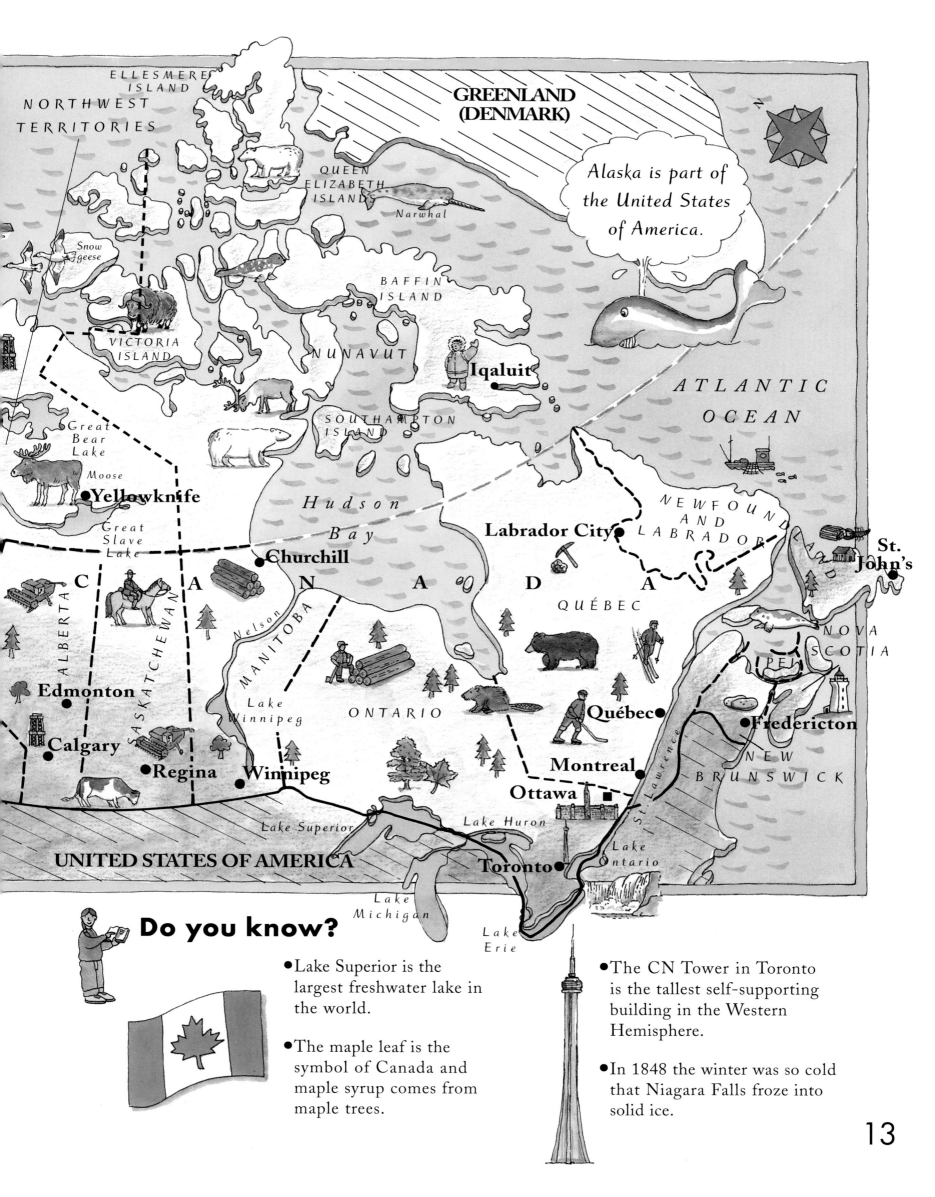

NORTHWEST TERRITORIES

ELLESMERE ISLAND

GREENLAND (DENMARK)

Alaska is part of the United States of America.

QUEEN ELIZABETH ISLANDS

Narwhal

BAFFIN ISLAND

NUNAVUT

Iqaluit

VICTORIA ISLAND

Snow Geese

Great Bear Lake

Moose

Yellowknife

Great Slave Lake

SOUTHAMPTON ISLAND

Hudson Bay

ATLANTIC OCEAN

NEWFOUNDLAND AND LABRADOR

Labrador City

St. John's

C   A   N

Churchill

A   D   A

QUÉBEC

ALBERTA

SASKATCHEWAN

MANITOBA

Nelson

Lake Winnipeg

ONTARIO

NOVA SCOTIA

P.E.I.

Edmonton

Calgary

Regina

Winnipeg

Québec

Fredericton

NEW BRUNSWICK

St. Lawrence

Montreal

Ottawa

Lake Superior

Lake Huron

Lake Ontario

Toronto

UNITED STATES OF AMERICA

Lake Michigan

Lake Erie

Do you know?

- Lake Superior is the largest freshwater lake in the world.

- The maple leaf is the symbol of Canada and maple syrup comes from maple trees.

- The CN Tower in Toronto is the tallest self-supporting building in the Western Hemisphere.

- In 1848 the winter was so cold that Niagara Falls froze into solid ice.

13

UNITED STATES OF AMERICA

Native Americans were the first people to live in this huge country. Now people from all over the world live here too. Most people work in factories and offices in big cities. There are many farms, including huge cattle ranches and wheat farms on the prairies. There is still plenty of space for wild animals in the mountains, deserts, forests and rivers.

Can you see?

The Golden Gate Bridge

The U.S. Capitol

The Statue of Liberty

a Pueblo Indian pot

a Mississippi steamboat

an American football player

a jazz singer

The Grand Canyon

a dinosaur fossil

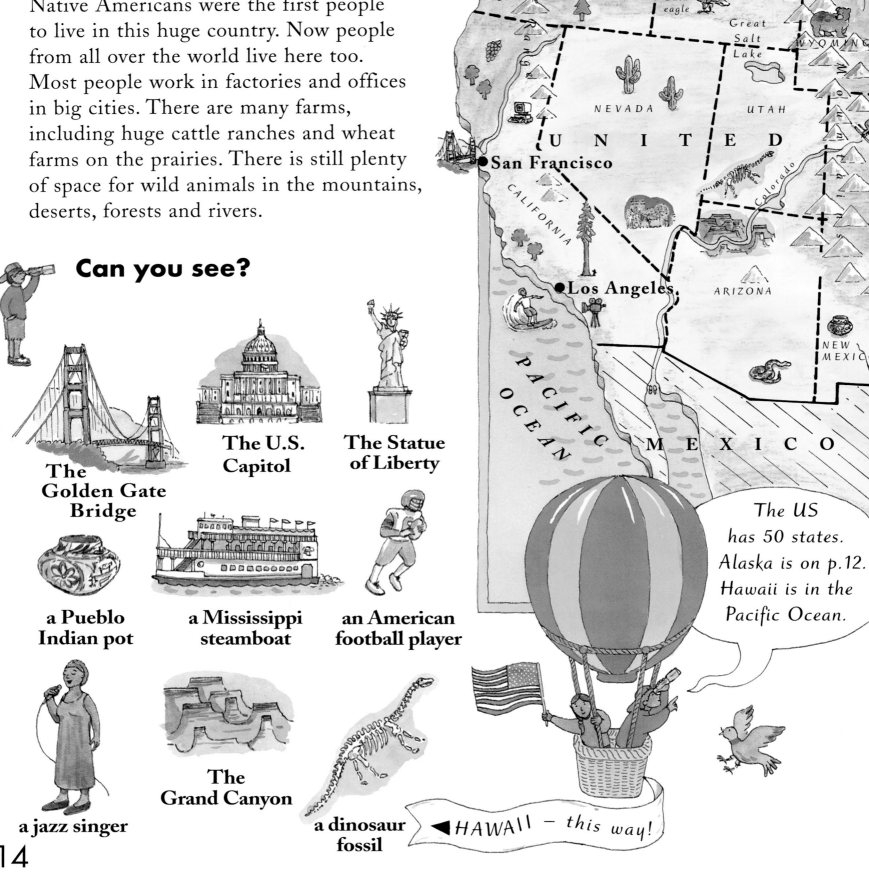

The US has 50 states. Alaska is on p.12. Hawaii is in the Pacific Ocean.

◄ HAWAII – this way!

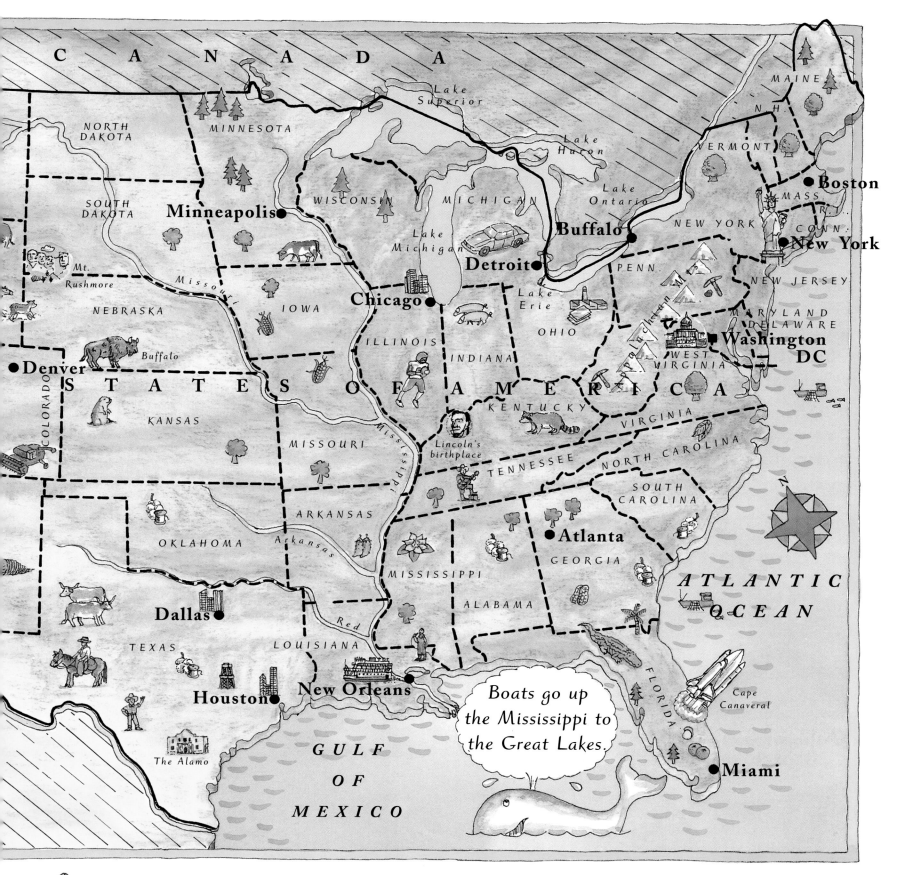

CANADA

Lake Superior

NORTH DAKOTA

MINNESOTA

SOUTH DAKOTA

Minneapolis

Lake Huron

MAINE

N.H.

VERMONT

Lake Ontario

Boston

MASS.

R.I.

WISCONSIN

MICHIGAN

Lake Michigan

Buffalo

NEW YORK

CONN.

New York

Detroit

P.E.N.N.

NEW JERSEY

Mt. Rushmore

Missouri

IOWA

Chicago

Lake Erie

OHIO

MARYLAND

DELAWARE

NEBRASKA

ILLINOIS

INDIANA

WEST VIRGINIA

Washington DC

Denver

Buffalo

S T A T E S   O F   A M E R I C A

COLORADO

KANSAS

MISSOURI

Mississippi

Lincoln's birthplace

KENTUCKY

VIRGINIA

NORTH CAROLINA

TENNESSEE

ARKANSAS

Arkansas

SOUTH CAROLINA

OKLAHOMA

MISSISSIPPI

Atlanta

GEORGIA

N

A T L A N T I C   O C E A N

ALABAMA

Dallas

Red

TEXAS

LOUISIANA

FLORIDA

Cape Canaveral

Houston

New Orleans

> Boats go up the Mississippi to the Great Lakes.

Miami

The Alamo

G U L F   O F   M E X I C O

Do you know?

- The heads of 4 great American presidents are carved into Mount Rushmore.

- A giant sequoia is the most massive tree in the world. It can grow as tall as a 28-floor building.

- Potato chips were invented by a Native American called George Crumm.

15

CENTRAL AMERICA

Central America is a bridge of land between North and South America. Thick rainforest covers the sides of the mountains. Most people are farmers. They grow coffee, sugar and fruit.

Tropical fruits, sugar and spices also grow well on the beautiful islands of the Caribbean. Tourists come here to enjoy the hot sunshine, the sea and the happy Caribbean music.

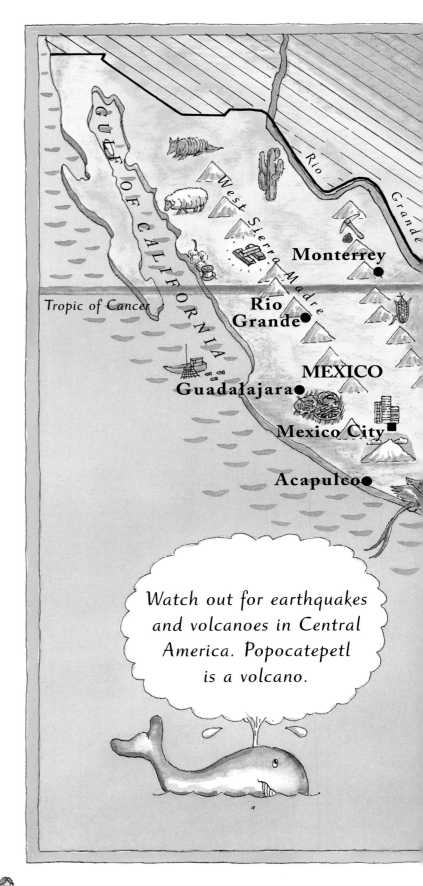

Watch out for earthquakes and volcanoes in Central America. Popocatepetl is a volcano.

Can you see?

Popocatepetl

an ancient Mayan city

Panama Canal

Mexican folk dancers

a steel band

a cricket player

a coral reef

a scuba diver

a quetzal

an armadillo

Do you know?

• The capital, Mexico City, is the largest Spanish-speaking city in the world.

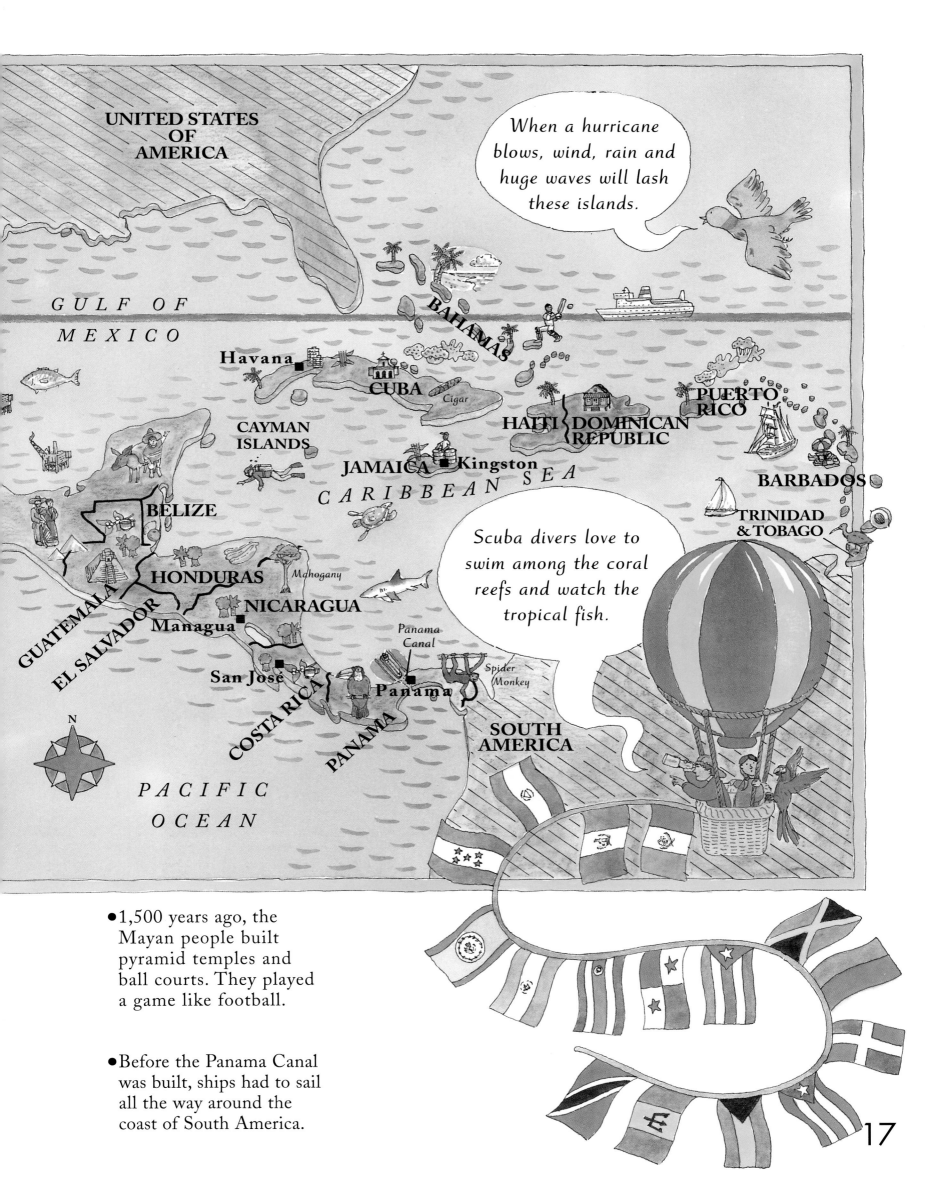

When a hurricane blows, wind, rain and huge waves will lash these islands.

Scuba divers love to swim among the coral reefs and watch the tropical fish.

UNITED STATES OF AMERICA

GULF OF MEXICO

Havana

CUBA

Cigar

CAYMAN ISLANDS

BAHAMAS

HAITI

DOMINICAN REPUBLIC

PUERTO RICO

BARBADOS

JAMAICA   Kingston

CARIBBEAN SEA

TRINIDAD & TOBAGO

BELIZE

GUATEMALA

HONDURAS

Mahogany

EL SALVADOR

Managua

NICARAGUA

San José

COSTA RICA

Panama Canal

Panama

Spider Monkey

SOUTH AMERICA

PANAMA

PACIFIC OCEAN

N

- 1,500 years ago, the Mayan people built pyramid temples and ball courts. They played a game like football.

- Before the Panama Canal was built, ships had to sail all the way around the coast of South America.

17

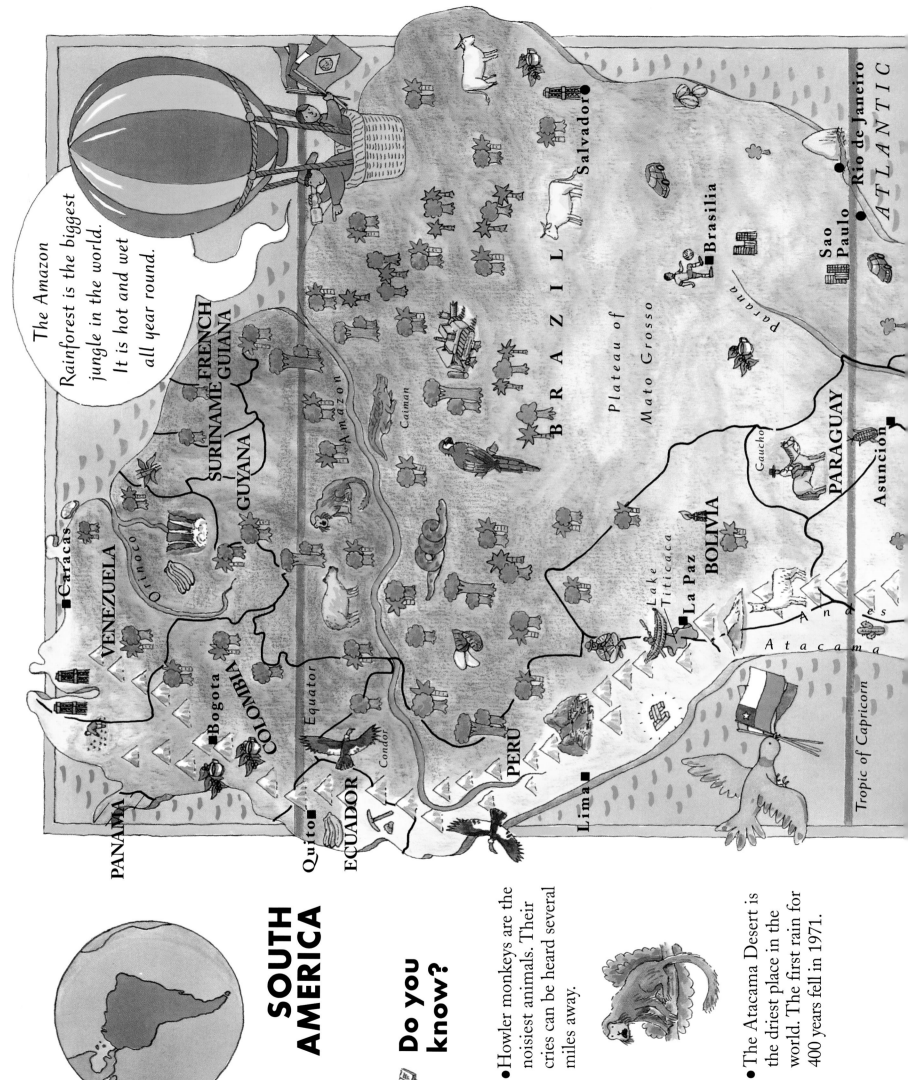

SOUTH AMERICA

The Amazon Rainforest is the biggest jungle in the world. It is hot and wet all year round.

Do you know?

- Howler monkeys are the noisiest animals. Their cries can be heard several miles away.

- The Atacama Desert is the driest place in the world. The first rain for 400 years fell in 1971.

PANAMA

VENEZUELA

Caracas

COLOMBIA

Bogota

Orinoco

ECUADOR

Quito

Equator

Condor

PERU

Lima

GUYANA

SURINAME

FRENCH GUIANA

Amazon

Caiman

B R A Z I L

Salvador

Brasilia

Plateau of Mato Grosso

Paraná

Sao Paulo

Rio de Janeiro

ATLANTIC

Lake Titicaca

La Paz

BOLIVIA

Gaucho

PARAGUAY

Asuncion

Andes

Atacama

Tropic of Capricorn

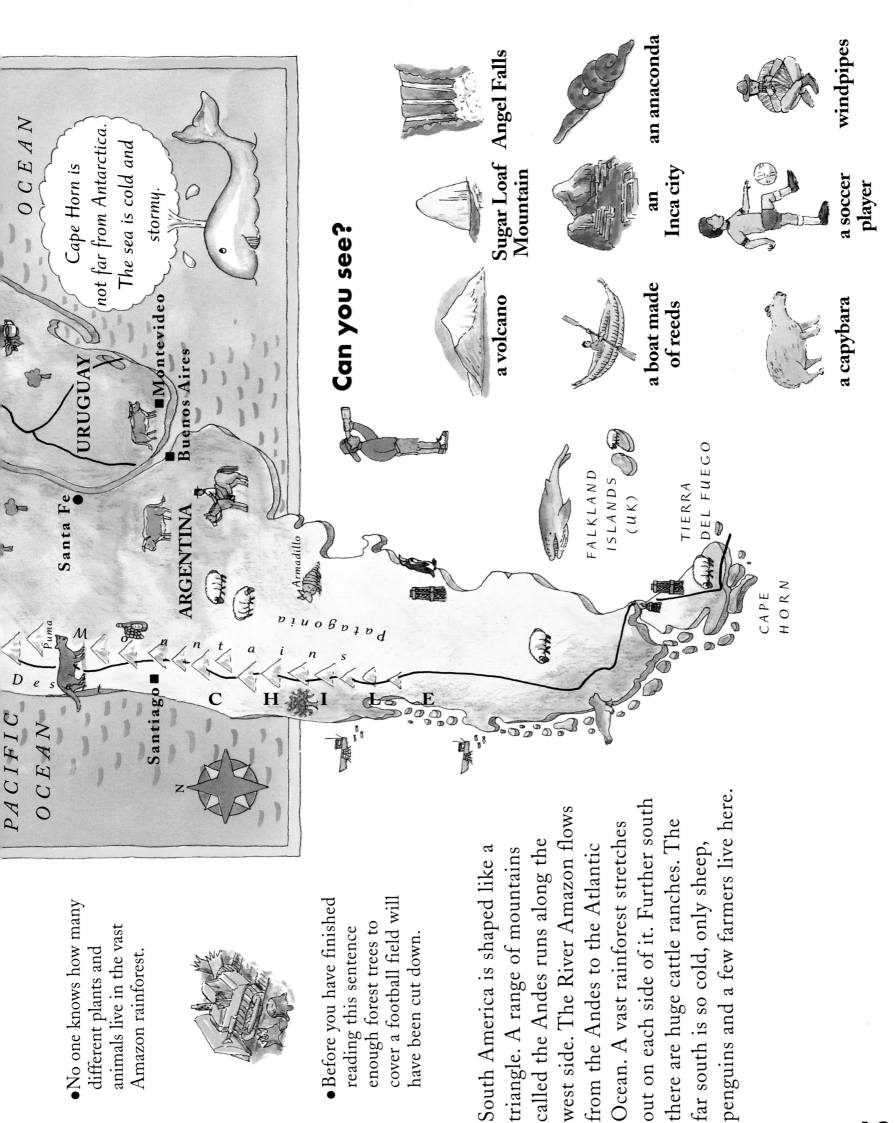

Cape Horn is not far from Antarctica. The sea is cold and stormy.

PACIFIC OCEAN

OCEAN

URUGUAY

Montevideo

Buenos Aires

Santa Fe

ARGENTINA

Santiago

C H I L E

Des *M* *t* *o* *u* *n* *t* *a* *i* *n* *s*

Puma

Armadillo

Patagonia

FALKLAND ISLANDS (UK)

TIERRA DEL FUEGO

CAPE HORN

N

Can you see?

Angel Falls

Sugar Loaf Mountain

an Inca city

an anaconda

a volcano

a boat made of reeds

a soccer player

windpipes

a capybara

• No one knows how many different plants and animals live in the vast Amazon rainforest.

• Before you have finished reading this sentence enough forest trees to cover a football field will have been cut down.

South America is shaped like a triangle. A range of mountains called the Andes runs along the west side. The River Amazon flows from the Andes to the Atlantic Ocean. A vast rainforest stretches out on each side of it. Further south there are huge cattle ranches. The far south is so cold, only sheep, penguins and a few farmers live here.

19

WESTERN EUROPE

Much of the land in Western Europe is used for farming, but most people live in towns and cities. Many cities are hundreds of years old. People come from all over the world to see the historic buildings. The countries around the Mediterranean are hot and sunny in summer. Then the beaches are crowded with sunbathers, windsurfers and sailboats.

Can you see?

The Colosseum

a gondolier

The Eiffel Tower

a Flamenco dancer

a windmill

Channel Tunnel

a castle on the Loire

Leaning Tower of Pisa

Mount Etna

REPUBLIC OF IRELAND

The English Channel is busy with big ships and small boats.

ATLANTIC OCEAN

The world's most famous wines come from France. Fine wines are made in Spain, Italy and Germany too.

Lisbon

PORTUGAL

NORTH SEA

DENMARK

■ Dublin

UNITED KINGDOM

NETHERLANDS

Hamburg

Berlin

POLAND

Brandenburg Gate

Amsterdam
Rotterdam

London ■

ENGLISH CHANNEL

Brussels
BELGIUM
Lille

Cologne
Bonn

Rhine

Elbe

GERMANY

CZECH REPUBLIC

SLOVAKIA

Vienna ■

Paris ■

LUX-EMBOURG

Seine

Munich

Danube

AUSTRIA

HUNGARY

Rennes ●

FRANCE

Loire

Zurich
Bern ■
SWITZERLAND
Geneva ●

Lake Geneva

A l p s

SLOVENIA

Venice ●

Bordeaux ●

Garonne

Lyons ●

Rhône

Turin ●
Po

Milan ●

A p e n n i n e s

A D R I A T I C   S E A

BOSNIA AND HERZEGOVINA

Florence ●

Bilbao ●

Ibex

P y r e n e e s

Wild boar

MONACO

Marseille ●

Rome ■

Naples ● **ITALY**

Ebro

ANDORRA
● Barcelona

C O R S I C A (FRANCE)

Pizza

SPAIN

Madrid ■

Tagus

Olive tree

Paella

BALEARIC ISLANDS (SPAIN)

S A R D I N I A (ITALY)

Mt. Etna

● Seville

The Alhambra

M E D I T E R R A N E A N   S E A

S I C I L Y (ITALY)

GIBRALTAR
Rock of Gibraltar

MALTA

Do you know?

- For nearly 50 years Germany was divided into two countries.

- The Vatican in Rome is the smallest country in the world. The Pope lives there.

- The French TGV is a very fast passenger train. It is twice as fast as an ordinary train.

- The St Gotthard tunnel is the third longest road tunnel in the world. It goes right under the Alps.

21

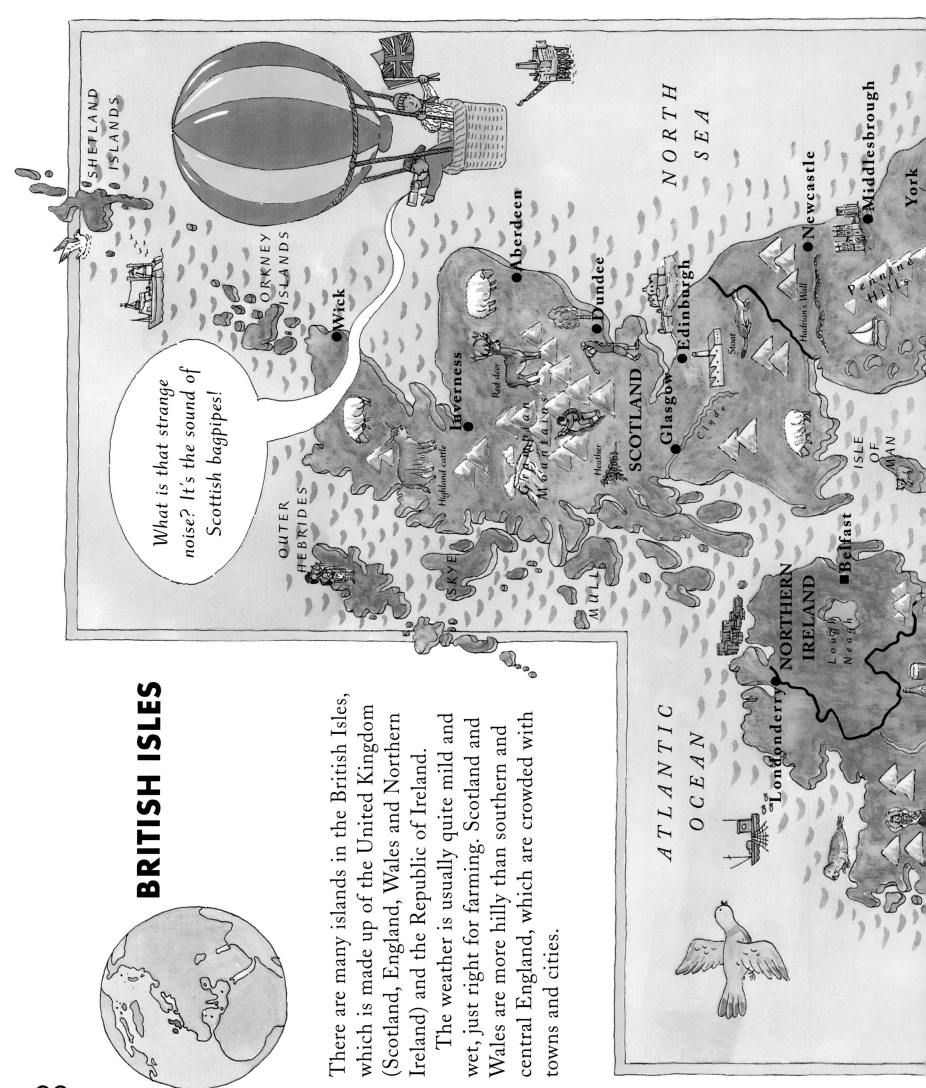

BRITISH ISLES

There are many islands in the British Isles, which is made up of the United Kingdom (Scotland, England, Wales and Northern Ireland) and the Republic of Ireland.

The weather is usually quite mild and wet, just right for farming. Scotland and Wales are more hilly than southern and central England, which are crowded with towns and cities.

What is that strange noise? It's the sound of Scottish bagpipes!

SHETLAND ISLANDS

ORKNEY ISLANDS

Wick

OUTER HEBRIDES

SKYE

MULL

Inverness

Red deer

Highland cattle

Grampian Mountains

Heather

Aberdeen

Dundee

Edinburgh

Stoat

SCOTLAND

Glasgow

Clyde

Hadrian's Wall

Pennine Hills

Newcastle

Middlesbrough

York

NORTH SEA

ISLE OF MAN

Belfast

NORTHERN IRELAND

Lough Neagh

Londonderry

ATLANTIC OCEAN

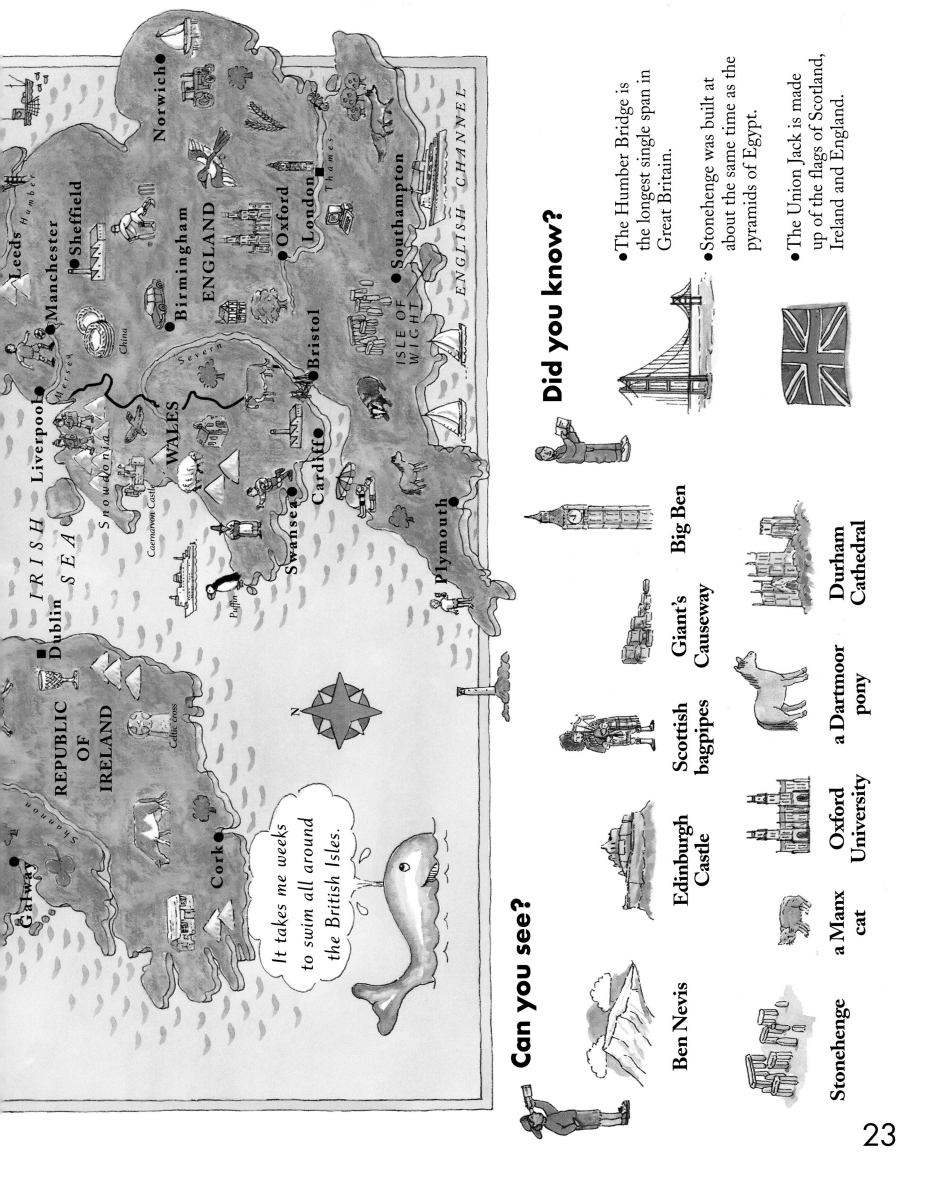

It takes me weeks to swim all around the British Isles.

Can you see?

Ben Nevis

a Manx cat

Stonehenge

Edinburgh Castle

Oxford University

Scottish bagpipes

a Dartmoor pony

Giant's Causeway

Big Ben

Durham Cathedral

Did you know?

- The Humber Bridge is the longest single span in Great Britain.

- Stonehenge was built at about the same time as the pyramids of Egypt.

- The Union Jack is made up of the flags of Scotland, Ireland and England.

23

EASTERN EUROPE

Most of Eastern Europe is covered with rugged mountains and forests. Only Poland and the land around the great Danube River is flat. Farmers here grow grapes, potatoes and other crops. They keep pigs, geese and cows. Barges and ships carry goods through Eastern Europe along the Danube. Winter is cold and snowy in the north, but the south is much warmer.

Can you see?

Warsaw Palace of Culture

Cathedral of St Vitus

The Parthenon

a barge

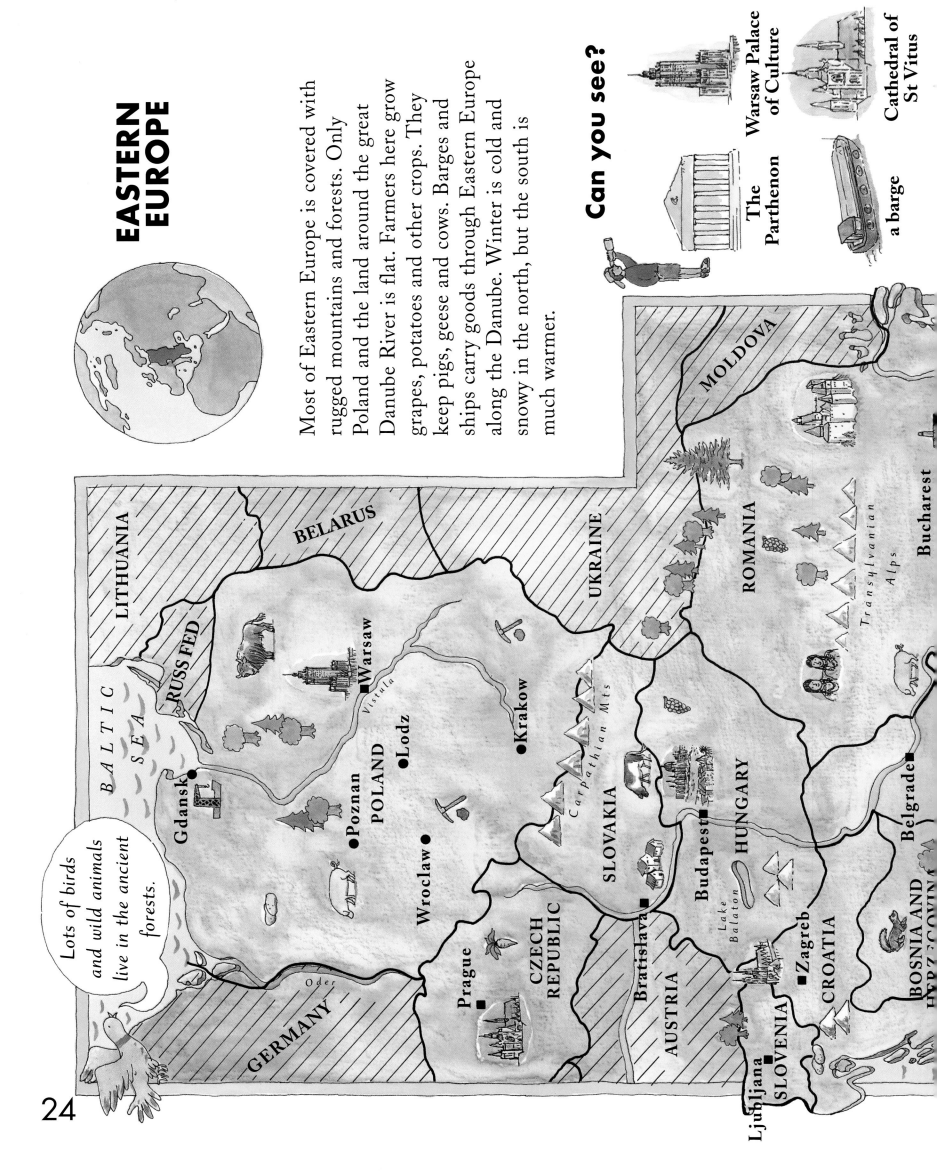

Lots of birds and wild animals live in the ancient forests.

GERMANY

BALTIC SEA

LITHUANIA

RUSS FED

BELARUS

UKRAINE

MOLDOVA

Gdansk

Poznan

POLAND

Lodz

Wroclaw

Warsaw

Vistula

Krakow

Oder

Prague

CZECH REPUBLIC

Bratislava

SLOVAKIA

Carpathian Mts

AUSTRIA

Budapest

HUNGARY

Lake Balaton

SLOVENIA

Ljubljana

Zagreb

CROATIA

BOSNIA AND HERZEGOVINA

Belgrade

ROMANIA

Transylvanian Alps

Bucharest

24

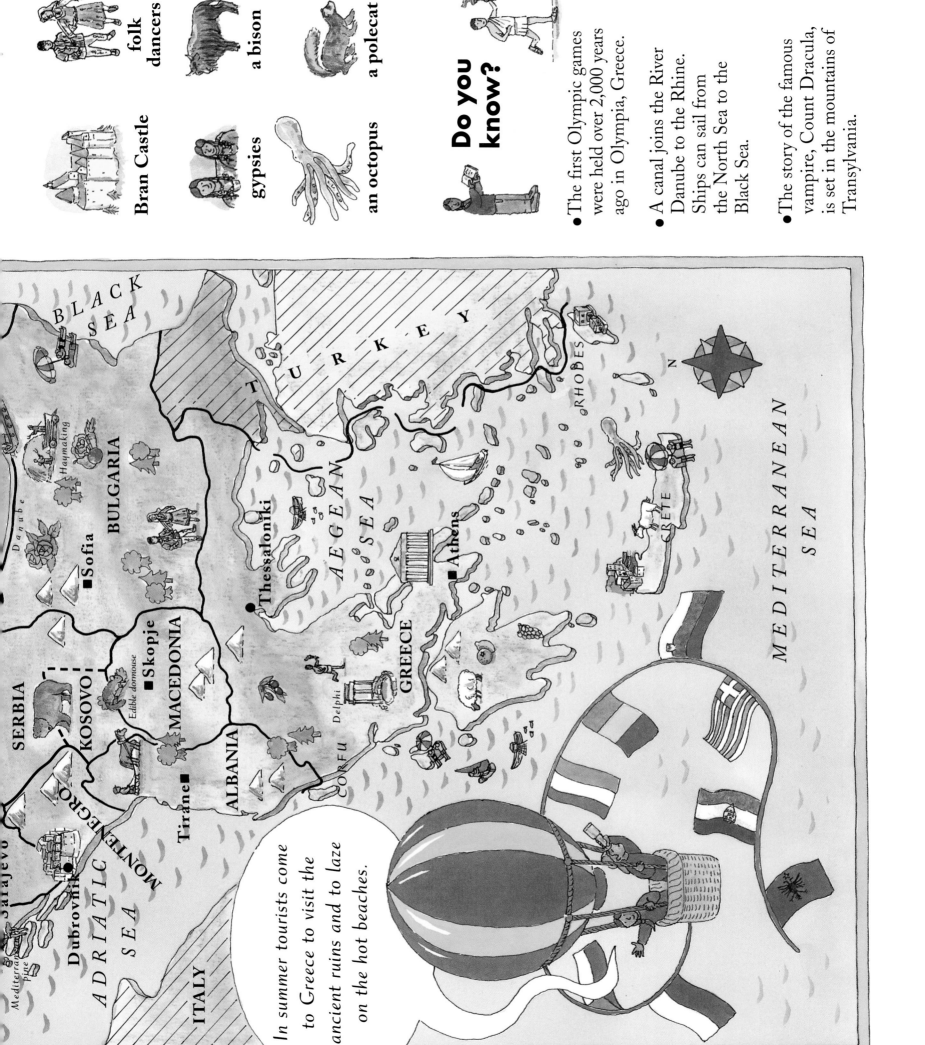

Bran Castle

folk dancers

a bison

gypsies

an octopus

a polecat

Do you know?

- The first Olympic games were held over 2,000 years ago in Olympia, Greece.

- A canal joins the River Danube to the Rhine. Ships can sail from the North Sea to the Black Sea.

- The story of the famous vampire, Count Dracula, is set in the mountains of Transylvania.

BLACK SEA

TURKEY

RHODES

AEGEAN SEA

MEDITERRANEAN SEA

Thessaloniki

Athens

Skopje

MACEDONIA

GREECE

Delphi

KOSOVO

SERBIA

Edible dormouse

Tiranë

ALBANIA

CORFU

MONTENEGRO

Dubrovnik

Sarajevo

ADRIATIC SEA

ITALY

Mediterranean Pine

BULGARIA

Sofia

Danube

Haymaking

CRETE

N

In summer tourists come to Greece to visit the ancient ruins and to laze on the hot beaches.

25

NORTHERN EUROPE

ICELAND

■ Reykjavik

Does Santa Claus really live in Lapland? Look, those Laplanders are using reindeer to pull their sledge.

Lakes and forests cover much of Northern Europe. The winters here are very cold, and people often use skis or sledges, as well as cars. Some of the trees are cut down to make timber and paper. Most people live in cities and on farms in the south. Many Norwegians work at sea, in fishing trawlers or on oil rigs.

Can you see?

 **Legoland**

 a Laplander

 **a cross-country skier**

 **a lemming**

 **a flying squirrel**

a paper mill

 **a fishing trawler**

 a Viking ship

 **a fjord**

Do you know?

- Hans Christian Andersen is Denmark's most famous writer. There is a bronze statue of his Little Mermaid in Copenhagen harbour.

- Hot water from Iceland's geysers provides central heating to the homes of Reykjavik.

- Lapland (in the far north) is called the Land of the Midnight Sun because it is light all night in summer.

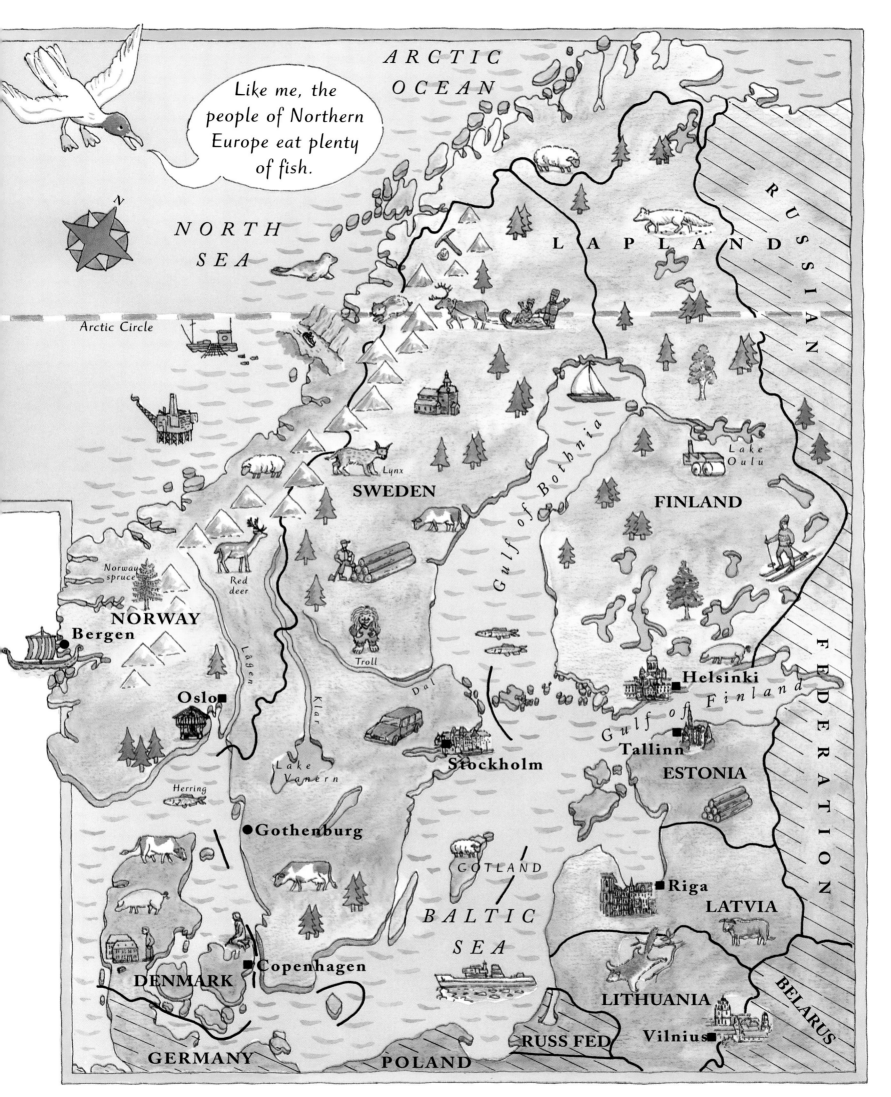

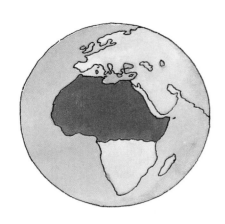

NORTHERN AFRICA

The vast Sahara Desert stretches across Northern Africa. Most people live south of the desert and around the coast. The land from Senegal to Cameroon used to be jungle but most of the trees have been cut down and crops such as coffee, cocoa and peanuts are grown instead.

Can you see?

an oasis

the Great mosque at Mali

a house made of mud and straw

drums

a scorpion

cocoa pods

yams

a Tuareg child

an oil well

a jerboa

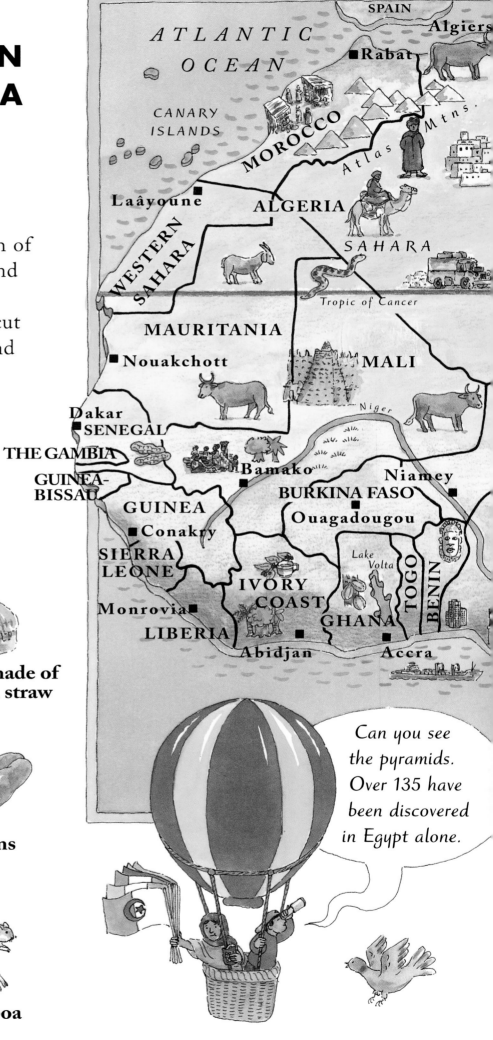

Can you see the pyramids. Over 135 have been discovered in Egypt alone.

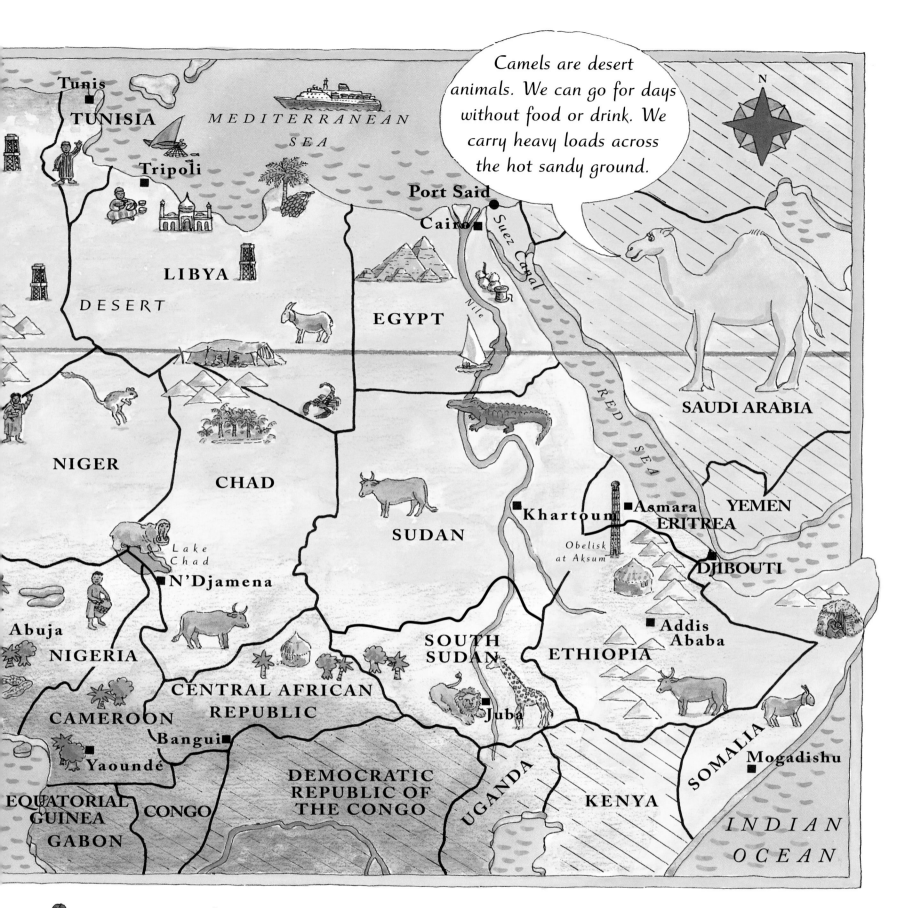

Do you know?

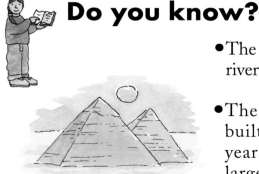

- The Nile is the longest river in the world.

- The pyramids were built around 4,000 years ago and are the largest stone buildings in the world.

- The Sahara is the world's hottest desert and is the largest subtropical desert in the world.

- The desert is scorching hot during the day and cold at night.

SOUTH AFRICA

Much of Southern Africa is high and flat. Farmers herd cattle on the grassy land in the East. Ferries and fishing boats sail on the big lakes. Giraffes and other wild animals live in the national parks. In the west, the Congo flows through thick rainforest. Few people live in the deserts of Namibia and the Kalahari, but many work in the gold, diamond and copper mines.

Can you see?

Victoria Falls

Great Zimbabwe

Mount Kilimanjaro

Kariba Dam

a Masai farmer

a lemur

a black rhino

diamonds

an athlete

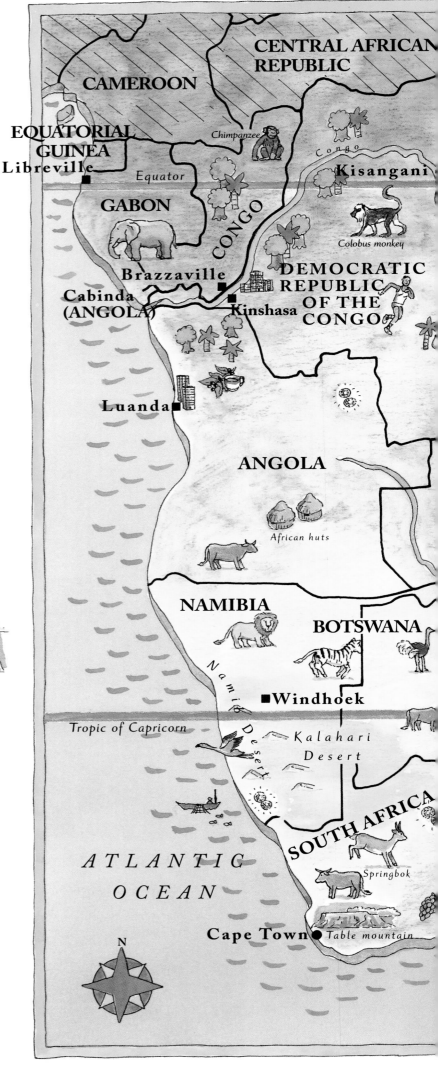

CAMEROON

CENTRAL AFRICAN REPUBLIC

EQUATORIAL GUINEA
Libreville

Chimpanzee

Equator

Congo

Kisangani

GABON

CONGO

Colobus monkey

Brazzaville

DEMOCRATIC REPUBLIC OF THE CONGO

Cabinda (ANGOLA)

Kinshasa

Luanda

ANGOLA

African huts

NAMIBIA

BOTSWANA

Namib Desert

Windhoek

Tropic of Capricorn

Kalahari Desert

SOUTH AFRICA

ATLANTIC OCEAN

Springbok

N

Cape Town

Table mountain

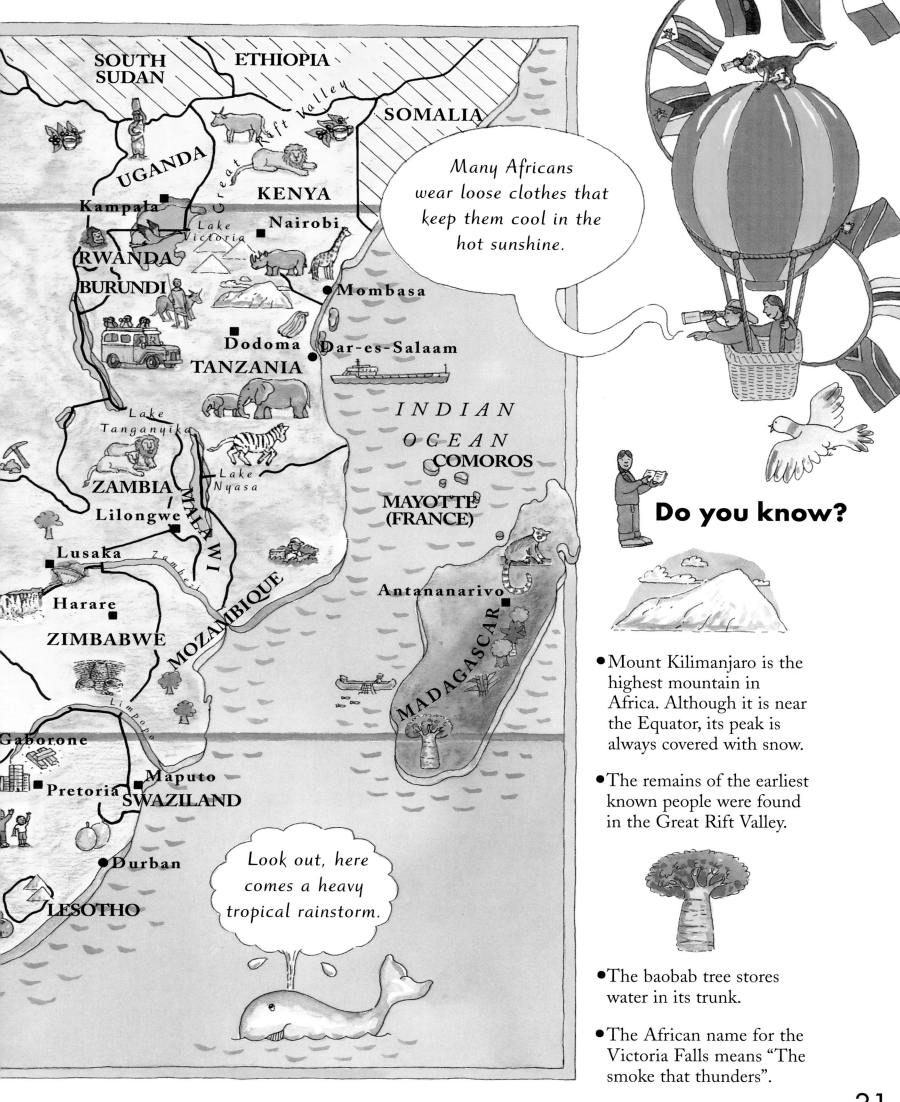

SOUTH SUDAN

ETHIOPIA

SOMALIA

UGANDA

Kampala

KENYA

Nairobi

RWANDA

BURUNDI

Lake Victoria

Great Rift Valley

Dodoma

Mombasa

Dar-es-Salaam

TANZANIA

Lake Tanganyika

INDIAN OCEAN

Lake Nyasa

COMOROS

ZAMBIA

Lilongwe

MALAWI

MAYOTTE (FRANCE)

Lusaka

Zambezi

Harare

ZIMBABWE

MOZAMBIQUE

Antananarivo

MADAGASCAR

Limpopo

Gaborone

Pretoria

Maputo

SWAZILAND

Durban

LESOTHO

Many Africans wear loose clothes that keep them cool in the hot sunshine.

Look out, here comes a heavy tropical rainstorm.

Do you know?

- Mount Kilimanjaro is the highest mountain in Africa. Although it is near the Equator, its peak is always covered with snow.

- The remains of the earliest known people were found in the Great Rift Valley.

- The baobab tree stores water in its trunk.

- The African name for the Victoria Falls means "The smoke that thunders".

RUSSIA AND NORTHERN ASIA

The Russian Federation is the largest of a group of countries sometimes called the CIS. Each country has its own language and customs, but most people also speak Russian. The Ural Mountains divide the Russian Federation. In the east, wolves, deer and bears roam vast pine forests and snowy wastes. Further south are grassy prairies. Most of the cities and farms are west and south of the Urals.

Europe and Asia meet at the Ural Mountains.

Can you see?

The Kremlin   The Winter Palace   Gateway at Samarkand

chess players   an elk   a sturgeon   Baikonur Cosmodrome

a troika   a Georgian dancer   a gold mine

Do you know?

• The Motherland statue was the largest in the world when it was completed in 1967. Her outstretched hand is large enough to hold an elephant.

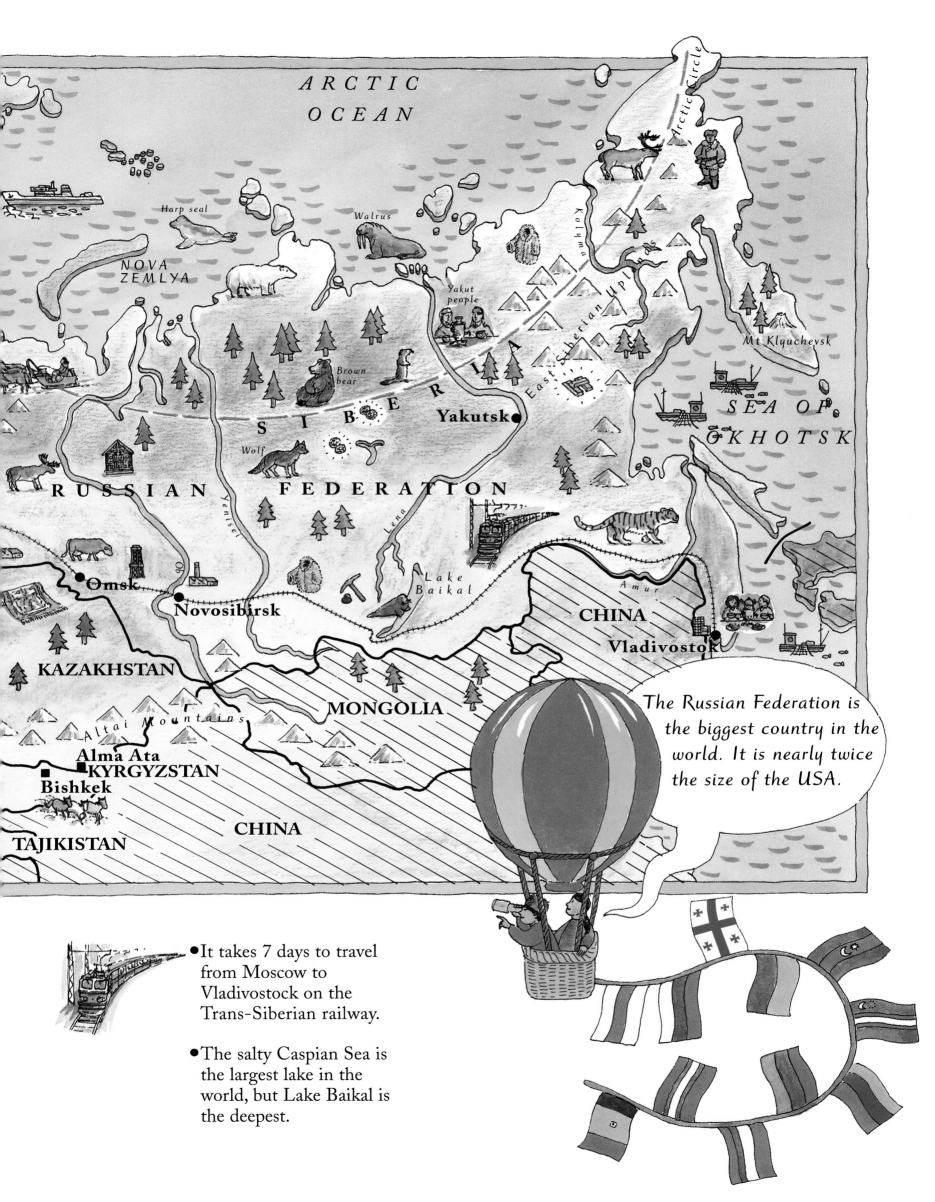

ARCTIC
OCEAN

Harp seal

Walrus

NOVA
ZEMLYA

Yakut
people

Mt Klyuchevsk

Brown
bear

SIBERIA

East Siberian Uplands

Yakutsk

SEA OF
OKHOTSK

Wolf

RUSSIAN   FEDERATION

Omsk

Novosibirsk

Lake
Baikal

Amur

CHINA

Vladivostok

KAZAKHSTAN

MONGOLIA

Altai Mountains

Alma Ata
KYRGYZSTAN

Bishkek

CHINA

TAJIKISTAN

The Russian Federation is
the biggest country in the
world. It is nearly twice
the size of the USA.

• It takes 7 days to travel
from Moscow to
Vladivostock on the
Trans-Siberian railway.

• The salty Caspian Sea is
the largest lake in the
world, but Lake Baikal is
the deepest.

SOUTHWEST ASIA

Hot deserts stretch from the Sahara and the Red Sea across Southwest Asia. Crops grow only where there is water, around oases and near rivers. Oil wells pump oil up from deep below the ground. Huge tankers carry it all around the world. Northern Iran and the countries around the Mediterranean Sea are cooler and have more rain, especially in winter.

Can you see?

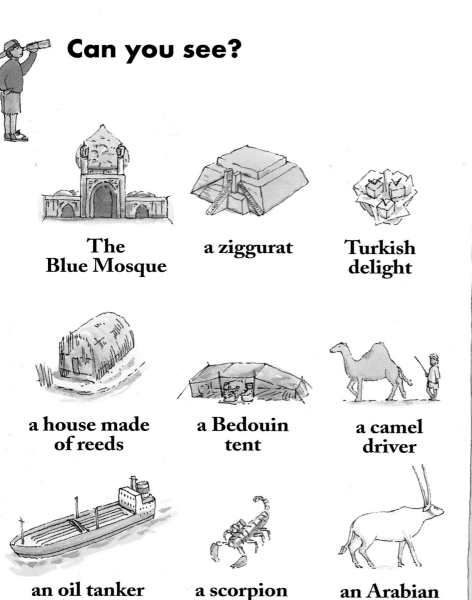

The Blue Mosque

a ziggurat

Turkish delight

a house made of reeds

a Bedouin tent

a camel driver

an oil tanker

a scorpion

an Arabian oryx

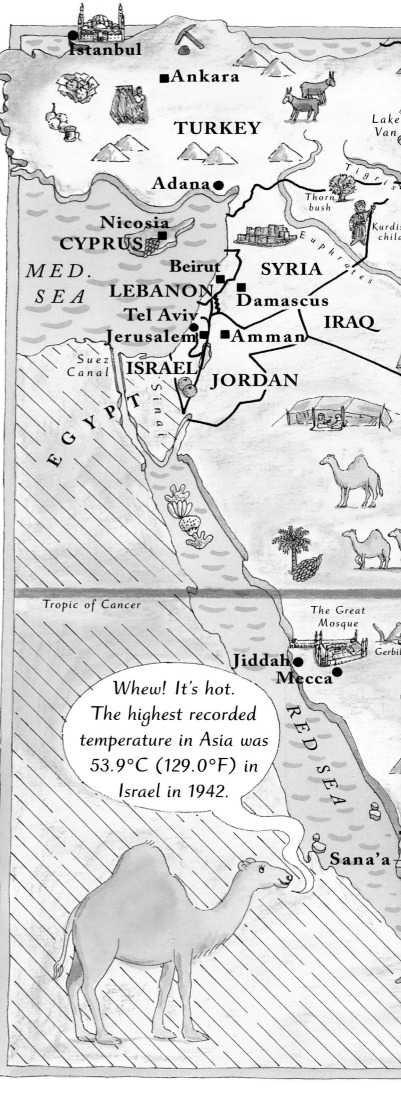

Istanbul

■Ankara

TURKEY

Lake Van

Adana ●

Thorn bush

Tigris

Kurdish child

Nicosia

CYPRUS

MED. SEA

Beirut

SYRIA

Euphrates

LEBANON

Damascus

Tel Aviv

IRAQ

Jerusalem

■Amman

Suez Canal

ISRAEL

JORDAN

E G Y P T

Sinai

Tropic of Cancer

The Great Mosque

Gerbil

Jiddah ●

Mecca ●

Whew! It's hot. The highest recorded temperature in Asia was 53.9°C (129.0°F) in Israel in 1942.

R E D S E A

Sana'a

34

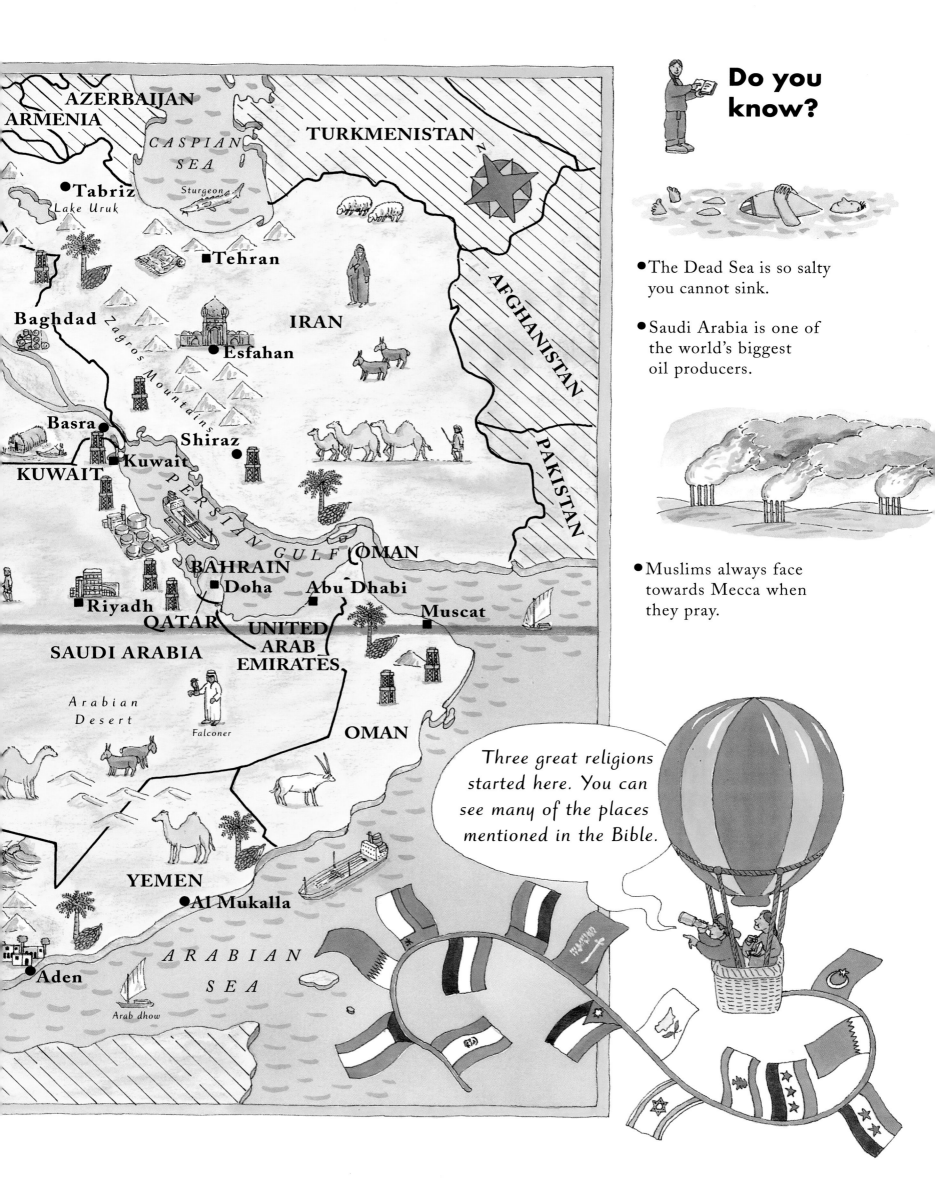

AZERBAIJAN

ARMENIA

CASPIAN SEA

Sturgeon

●Tabriz
Lake Uruk

TURKMENISTAN

N

AFGHANISTAN

PAKISTAN

■Tehran

IRAN

Baghdad

Zagros Mountains

●Esfahan

Basra

Shiraz

■Kuwait

KUWAIT

PERSIAN GULF

OMAN

BAHRAIN
■Doha
Abu Dhabi

■Muscat

■Riyadh

QATAR

UNITED ARAB EMIRATES

SAUDI ARABIA

OMAN

Arabian Desert

Falconer

YEMEN
●Al Mukalla

ARABIAN SEA

●Aden

Arab dhow

Do you know?

● The Dead Sea is so salty you cannot sink.

● Saudi Arabia is one of the world's biggest oil producers.

● Muslims always face towards Mecca when they pray.

Three great religions started here. You can see many of the places mentioned in the Bible.

SOUTHERN and SOUTHEAST ASIA

These countries lie close to the equator, so the weather is either hot and dry, or hot and wet and steamy. Thick rainforest covers the mountains and islands of the southeast, but much of it has been cleared by farmers. Most people farm around small villages. They have few machines to help them with their work. The cities bustle with people, bikes, cars and animals.

Can you see?

The Taj Mahal

The Golden Temple

Mount Everest

a Bactrian camel

a Buddhist monk

a sacred cow

a Hindu festival

a bus

a Komodo dragon

a monkey-eating eagle

a flying fish

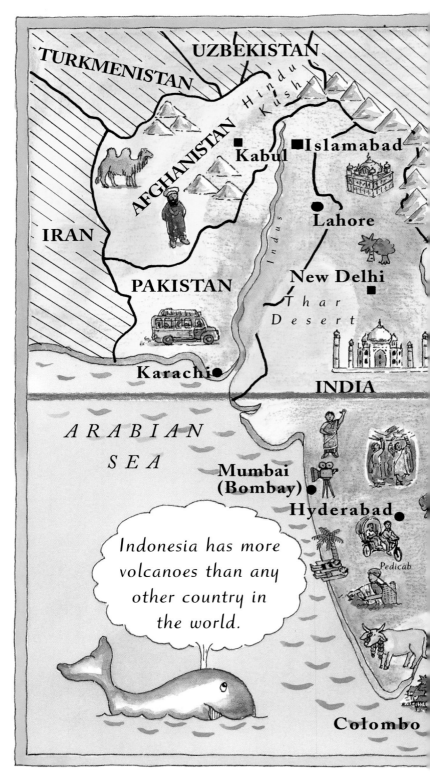

Indonesia has more volcanoes than any other country in the world.

Do you know?

- Mount Everest is the world's highest mountain. There are 96 other peaks in the Himalayas which are also very high.

- In the wet season, monsoon rains flood the land and the streets become like rivers.

- Hindus believe that the Ganges is a holy river. They travel there to bathe in the water.

36

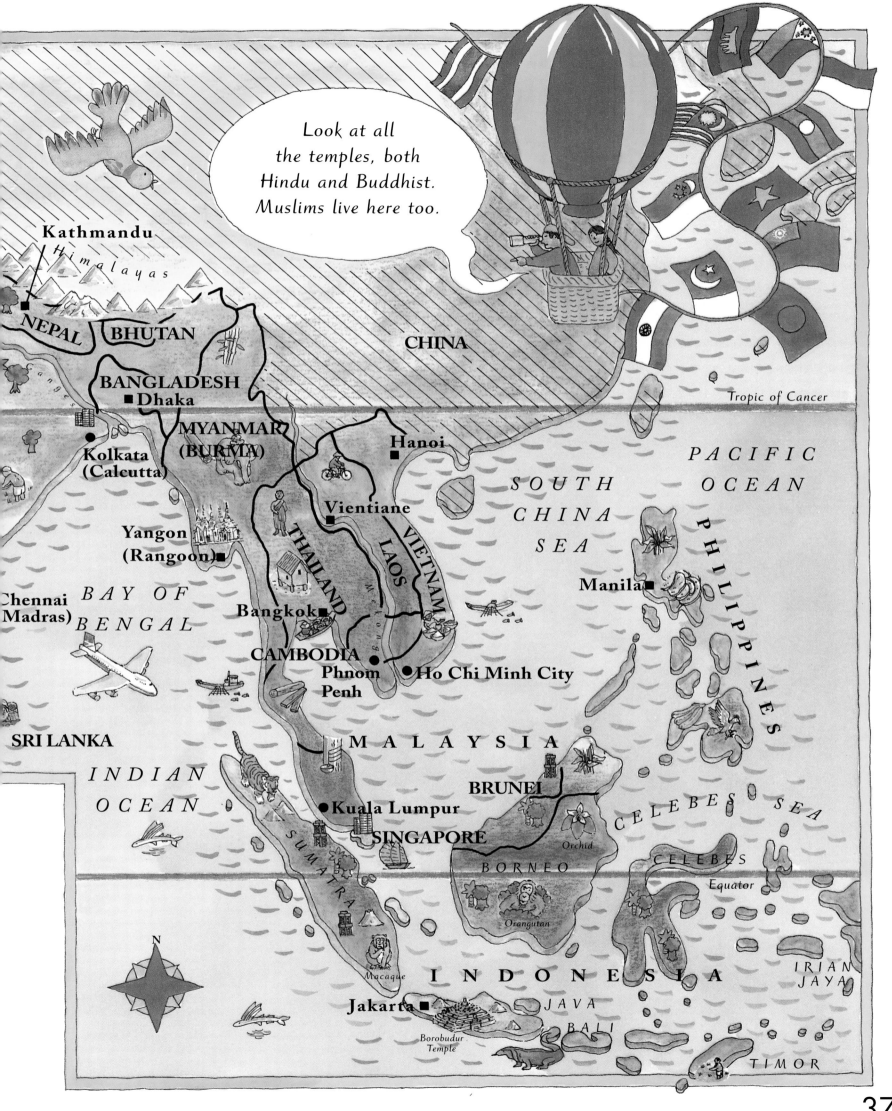

CHINA and JAPAN

China has more people than any other country, yet the land is mostly hot, empty desert or cold, high mountains. Most people live in villages on the flat plains in the east.

Japan is made up of several islands, with high mountains. Some of these are volcanoes. Most people live on narrow strips of land along the east coast. The cities are very crowded.

Can you see?

The Terracotta Army

The Great Buddha

The Temple of Heaven

The Potala Palace

Guilin Hills

a Japanese child

a Chinese dancer

a bicycle

a giant panda

a tiger

KAZAKHSTAN

KYRGYZSTAN

Japanese people do not shake hands – they bow instead.

Taklimakan Desert

Himalayas

Tibetan Plateau

TIBET

NEPAL

Lhasa

INDIA

Tropic of Cancer

There are very few pandas left. The bamboo we eat is disappearing fast.

BURMA

Did you know?

- Chinese and Japanese people eat their food with chopsticks.

- One fifth of the world's population lives in China.

38

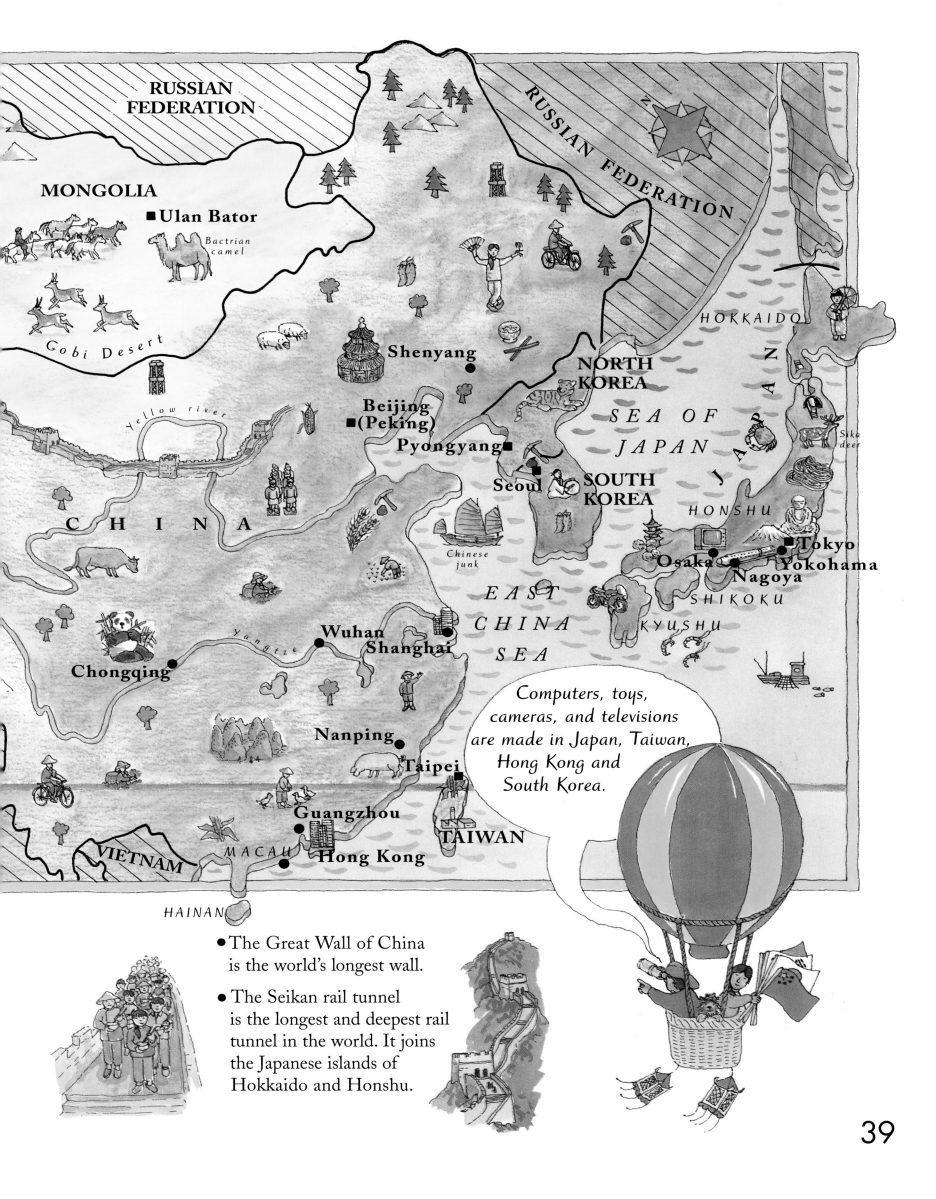

RUSSIAN FEDERATION

RUSSIAN FEDERATION

MONGOLIA

■Ulan Bator

Bactrian camel

Gobi Desert

Yellow river

Shenyang

Beijing (Peking)

Pyongyang

NORTH KOREA

Seoul

SOUTH KOREA

CHINA

HOKKAIDO

SEA OF JAPAN

HONSHU

J A P A N

Sika deer

Tokyo
Yokohama
Osaka
Nagoya

SHIKOKU

KYUSHU

Chongqing

Yangtze

Wuhan
Shanghai

Chinese junk

EAST CHINA SEA

Nanping

Taipei

TAIWAN

Guangzhou

MACAU

Hong Kong

VIETNAM

HAINAN

Computers, toys, cameras, and televisions are made in Japan, Taiwan, Hong Kong and South Korea.

- The Great Wall of China is the world's longest wall.

- The Seikan rail tunnel is the longest and deepest rail tunnel in the world. It joins the Japanese islands of Hokkaido and Honshu.

39

AUSTRALASIA

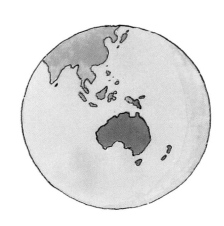

Australasia includes thousands of islands in the Pacific as well as Australia, New Zealand and Papua New Guinea. The north of Australia is tropical rainforest, but inland is flat desert. Most people live in cities around the coast.

Both Australia and New Zealand have big sheep and cattle farms. They also have wild animals that are found nowhere else in the world.

Do you know?

- Australia is the smallest continent in the world.

- The Great Barrier Reef is the longest coral reef. It is made of the shells of billions of tiny animals.

Can you see?

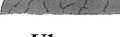
Uluru (Ayers rock)

Sydney Opera House

a boomerang

a surfer

an Aboriginal child

a cricket player

a rugby player

a flying doctor plane

a Maori dancer

a tuatara

- Uluru is a single huge outcrop of rock.

- The kiwi is the national symbol of New Zealand. It cannot fly and uses its long beak to stab the ground for worms.

INDIAN OCEAN

Darwin

Great Sandy Desert

Lake Mackay

A U S T R

Gibson Desert

WESTERN AUSTRALIA

Great Victoria Desert

Dingo

Perth

Gum tree

GREAT AUSTRALIAN BIGHT

We have moved New Zealand closer to Australia to get it on the map.

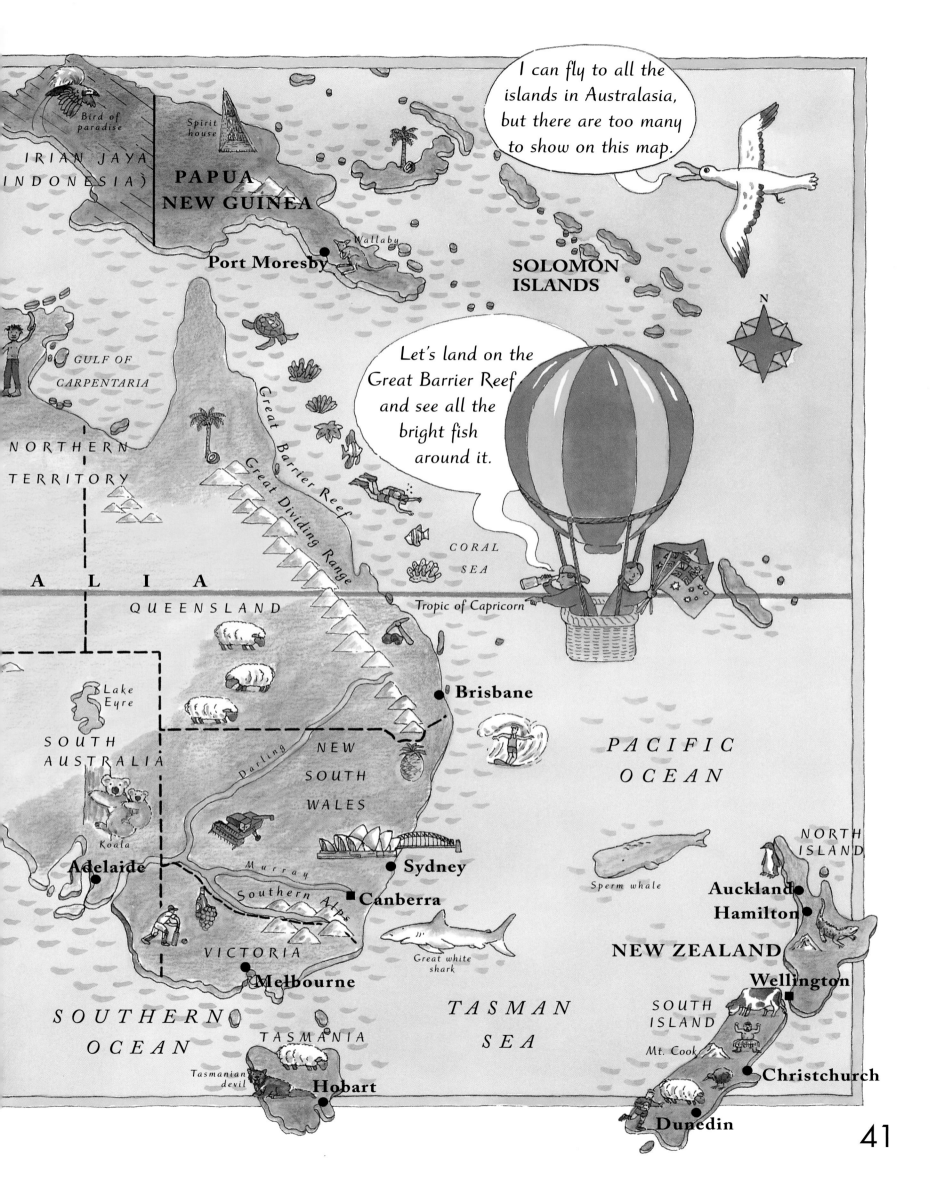

41

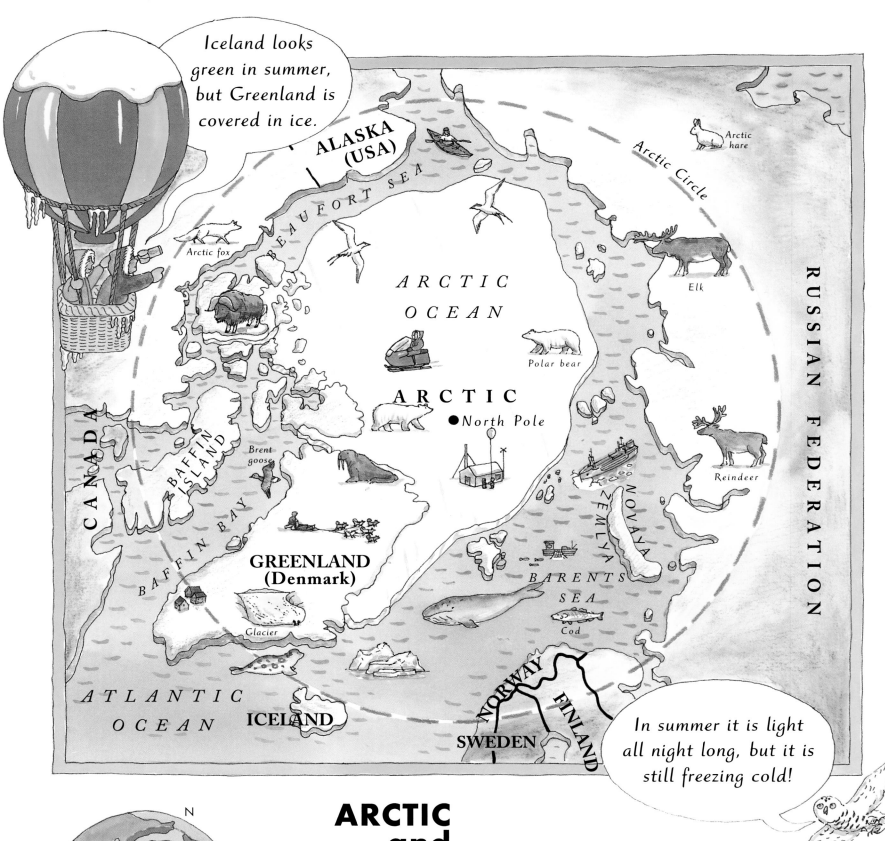

ARCTIC and ANTARCTIC

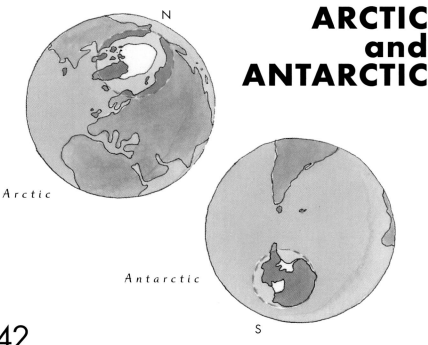

Arctic

Antarctic

The Arctic is an ocean of ice surrounded by land. Only summer is warm enough to melt some of the sea. The Antarctic is land surrounded by frozen sea. It is nearly twice as big as Australia but only seals and penguins live here all year round. No one owns this land and every country has agreed to preserve Antarctica as a wilderness.

Can you see?

a fish-factory
ship

an iceberg

a leopard seal

an Arctic tern

a musk ox

an explorer

a research
station

an Emperor
penguin

Do you know?

- The Arctic tern migrates between the Arctic and Antarctic. It sees more daylight than any other animal.

- Glaciers are rivers of ice. They move so slowly that it would take 3,000 years for a snowflake to travel from the middle of Greenland to the sea.

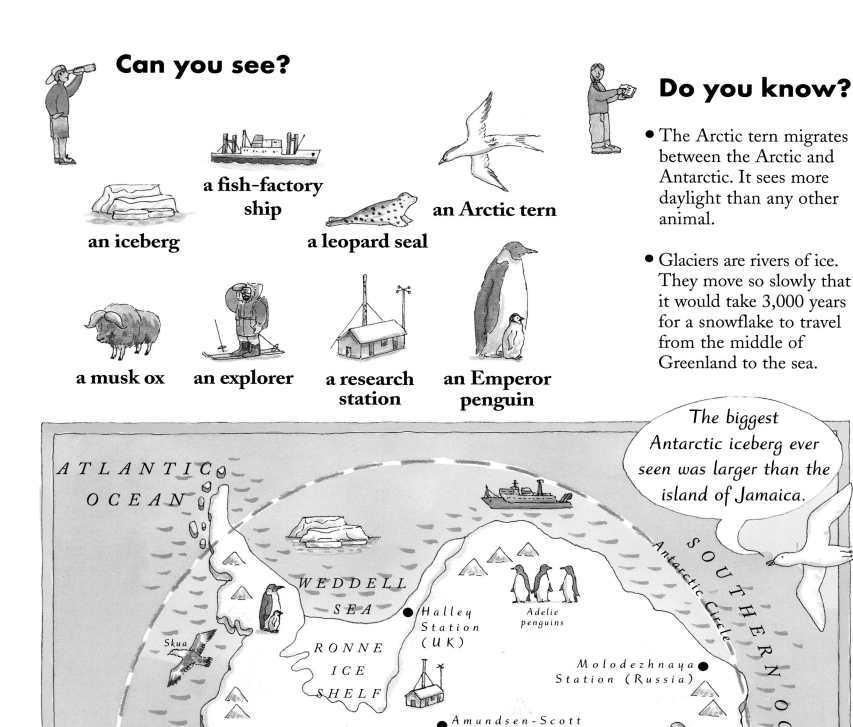

The biggest Antarctic iceberg ever seen was larger than the island of Jamaica.

ATLANTIC OCEAN

WEDDELL SEA

RONNE ICE SHELF

Halley Station (UK)

Adelie penguins

Molodezhnaya Station (Russia)

Skua

Amundsen-Scott Station (USA)

South Pole

ANTARCTICA

Vostok Station (Russia)

Scientists

ROSS ICE SHELF

SOUTH PACIFIC OCEAN

McMurdo Air Station (USA)

Casey Base (Australia)

Weddell seal

Dumont D'Urville Station (France)

INDIAN OCEAN

SOUTHERN OCEAN

Antarctic Circle

SOME FLAGS OF THE WORLD

 UK

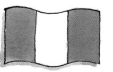 Rep. of Ireland

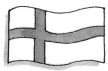 Denmark

 Finland

 Sweden

 Norway

 Iceland

 Netherlands

 Belgium

 Luxembourg

 Switzerland

 Austria

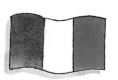 France

 Germany

 Italy

 Spain

 Portugal

 China

 Japan

 South Africa

 Malaysia

 Thailand

 India

 Pakistan

 Nepal

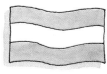 Indonesia

 Zambia

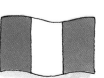 USA

 Canada

 Mexico

 Cuba

 Jamaica

 Argentina

 Brazil

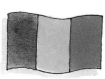 Peru

 Ecuador

 Colombia

 Chile

 Australia

 New Zealand

 Kenya

 Angola

 Guatemala

 Costa Rica

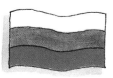 Panama

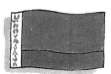 Poland

 Romania

 Hungary

 Algeria

 Zimbabwe

 Russian Federation

 Belarus

 Azerbaijan

 Georgia

 Estonia

 Greece

Israel

Laos

Jordan

Oman

44

COUNTRY INDEX

A

Afghanistan 32, 35, 36
Albania 25
Algeria 28
Andorra 21
Angola 30
Antarctica 43
Argentina 18, 19
Armenia 32, 33
Australia 40, 41
Austria 21, 24
Azerbaijan 32, 35

B

Bahamas 17
Bahrain 35
Bangladesh 37
Barbados 17
Belgium 21
Belize 17
Belarus 24, 32
Benin 28
Bermuda 17
Bhutan 37
Bolivia 18
Bosnia and Herzegovina 24
Botswana 30, 31
Brazil 18, 19
British Isles, 20, 22, 23
Brunei 37
Bulgaria 24, 25
Burkina Faso 28
Burma 37
Burundi 31

C

Cambodia 37
Cameroon 29, 30
Canada 12-15, 42
Central African
    Republic 29, 30
Chad 29
Chile 19
China 28, 29, 33, 37
Colombia 18
Congo 29, 30
Costa Rica 17
Croatia 24
Cuba 17
Cyprus 34
Czech Republic 21, 24

D

Denmark 21, 27
Democratic Republic
    of the Congo 29, 30
Djibouti 29
Dominican Republic 17

E

Ecuador 18
Egypt 29
El Salvador 17

England 20, 21, 23
Equatorial Guinea 38
Eritrea 29
Estonia 27
Ethiopia 29

F

Falkland Islands 19
Finland 27, 32
France 21
French Guiana 18

G

Gabon 29, 30
Gambia, the 28
Georgia 32
Germany 21, 25
Ghana 28
Gibraltar 28
Greece 24
Greenland 13, 42
Guatemala 17
Guinea 28
Guinea-Bissau 28
Guyana 18

H

Haiti 17
Honduras 17
Hong Kong, 39
Hungary 21, 24

I

Iceland 26, 42
India 36, 37
Indonesia 37, 40
Iran 35, 36
Iraq 34, 35
Ireland, Northern, 22
Ireland, Republic of, 20
Israel 34
Italy 21
Ivory Coast 20

J

Jamaica, 17
Japan 39
Jordan 34

K

Kakakhstan 32, 33
Kenya 29, 31
Kosovo 24, 25
Kuwait 35
Kyrgyzstan 33

L

Laos 37
Latvia 27
Lebanon 35
Lesotho 31
Liberia 28
Libya 29

Lithuania 25, 27
Luxembourg 21

M

Macedonia 25
Madagascar 31
Malawi 31
Malaysia 37
Mali 28
Mauritania 28
Mauritius 31
Mexico 14, 15, 16
Moldova 24
Monaco 21
Mongolia 33
Montenegro 24, 25
Morocco 28
Mozambique 31

N

Namibia 30
Nepal 37, 38
Netherlands 21
New Zealand 40, 41
Nicaragua 17
Niger 29
Nigeria 28, 29
North Korea 39
Norway 27, 42

O

Oman 35

P

Pakistan 35, 36
Panama 17
Papua New Guinea 41
Paraguay 18
Peru 18
Philippines 37
Poland 24, 27, 32
Portugal 20
Puerto Rico 17

Q

Qatar 35

R

Romania 24, 25, 32
Russian Federation
    27, 32, 33, 42
Rwanda 31

S

San Marino 21
Saudi Arabia 34, 35
Scotland 20
Senegal 28
Serbia 24, 25
Sierra Leone 28
Singapore 37
Slovakia 21, 25
Slovenia 21, 24

Solomon Islands 41
Somalia 29, 31
South Africa 30, 31
South Korea 39
South Sudan 29
Spain 20, 21
Sri Lanka 36, 37
Sudan 29, 31
Suriname 18
Swaziland 31
Sweden 24, 27, 42
Switzerland 21
Syria 34

T

Taiwan 39
Tajikstan 33
Tanzania 31
Thailand 37
Togo 28
Trinidad and Tobago 17
Tunisia 29
Turkey 25, 34
Turkmenistan 32, 35

U

Uganda 29, 31
Ukraine 24, 32
United Arab Emirates 35
United Kingdom 20-23
United States of
    America 12-15, 17, 42
Uruguay 19
Uzbekistan 32

V

Vatican City 21
Venezuela 18
Vietnam 37

W

Wales 20, 21, 23
Western Sahara 28

Y

Yemen 24, 29, 35

Z

Zambia 30, 31
Zimbabwe 30, 31

Look at all the countries we have visited!

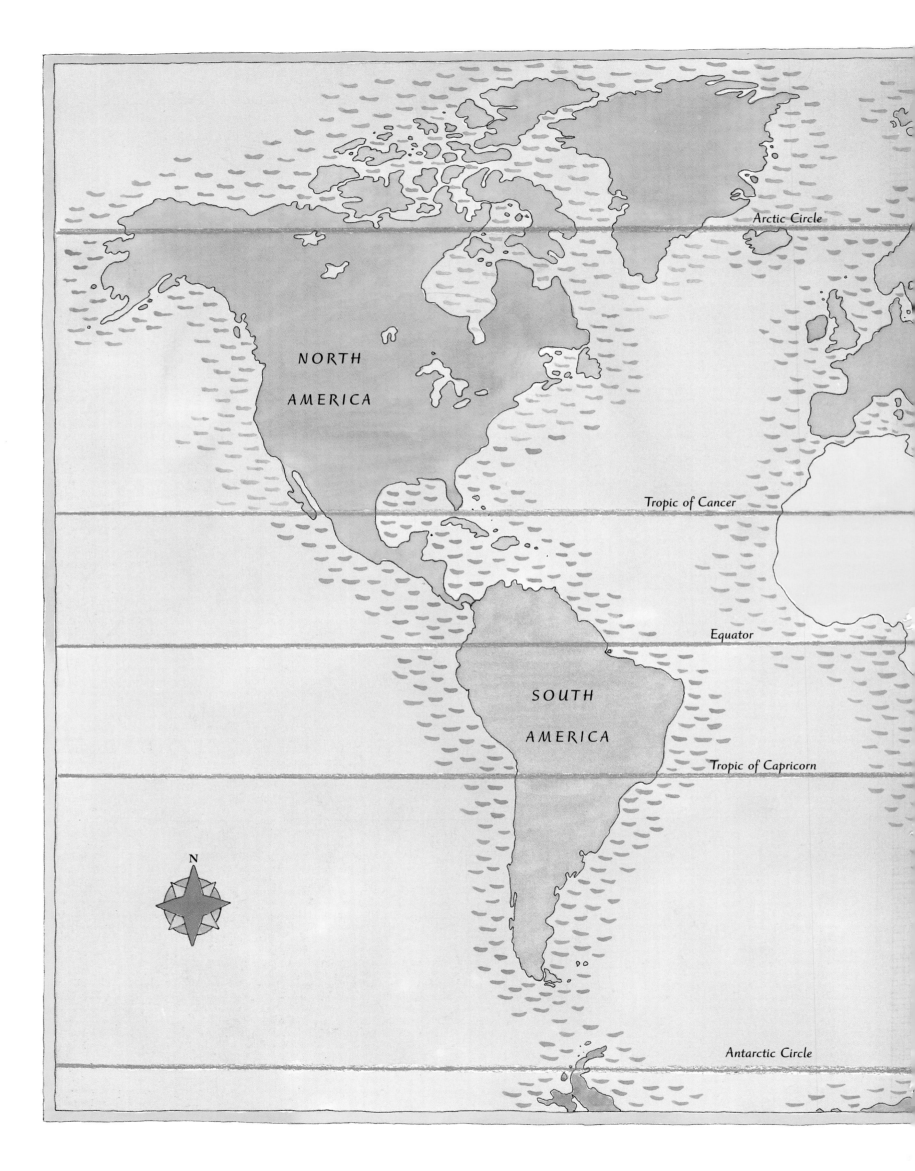